The Ultimate Moment No Regrets

Tamika Newhouse

Delphine Publications, LLC
9439 Everton
San Antonio, Texas 78245

ISBN-13: 978-0982145524
Library of Congress Control Number: 2009908203

First printing August 2009

Printed in the United States

www.delphinepublications.com
www.tamikanewhouse.com

Edited by. Docuversion

Cover design by Custom eyes studios

Praise for *The Ultimate* NO NO

A page-turner with lots of drama.

- APOOO

The Ultimate No No is a amazing piece of literature that will have you on the edge of your seat focusing only on what's gonna happen next, it is a real page turner

- AAMBC

The way the author introduces the characters in the story and tantalizes the reader with glimpses of their lives creates such an intensity that you just want more.

- Reading is what we do

Every page is laced with drama. The drama between friends, lovers, and the lies and secrets that surround them.

- Chick Lit. Gurl

As I closed the book I wondered about each character what they were doing and how life was treating them?

- Reader's Paradise

Riveting in Drama, Deceit, Lust, Love, Heartache & Forgiveness.

- Savvy Reviewers

Characters were practical and relatable, Newhouse knows one thing - drama!

- OOSA

Warning: Do not read at night, will cause insomnia.

_ Oasis, Author of Duplicity

Also By Tamika Newhouse

The Ultimate NO NO

Anthologies

A Reflection of Me: AAMBC Anthology
Bedtime Stories

Coming 2010

Cookie: A Fort Worth Story
Between the Sheets Anthology

For
Marckus, my other half, my sweetness.

Nitrah Hill

April 2004

Fuck no, this was not happening to me! Was Troy really sitting here agreeing that he was going to marry that dirty bitch? It hit me hard, hard like a slap to my face. Why would he marry her instead of me? I looked at her and rolled my eyes with all the sassiness I had.

Damn.

I thought the last time I would see Teresa was in Florida. Apparently she got around pretty quick. I couldn't stand the look on her face as she stood outside of Troy's car with her arms crossed and tapping her foot. I knew that Teresa wouldn't be happy to see her boyfriend sitting in the car with me, his ex. She knew me and Troy's history. Hell, everyone knew. I was the woman who was supposed to be wearing Troy's ring, or maybe even Denim's ring, but that's another story. Denim and I both had a problem when it came to a relationship together, neither one of us could stay faithful.

It sure seemed like I couldn't win at love. I wanted to punch Teresa and knock her down. I needed her to feel what I was feeling, which was embarrassed, hurt, and confused. It had been months since I'd seen or heard from Troy and when I did, he blindsided me with this news, after he said that he would always love me. Ugh, why did I have to do that stupid scam Dahlia wanted? I forgave her, but it was obvious that Troy couldn't forgive me. Better yet, why couldn't he just tell me that he was kidding? *Why didn't he say that he wanted to marry me and that Teresa was a clouded misjudgment?*

See it all started off when Dahlia came to me and a couple of our other friends about her secret. Dahlia had been my friend since college. Of course I thought that we had no secrets, but she revealed that her ex was Troy of all people. Back in college he had broken her heart; in return, she wanted me to break his.

How was I supposed to do that? Simple. I was to date him, make him fall in love with me, and then dump him. In retrospect, it was a no-win situation, especially since I fell in love with him. He fell hard for me, too. Now of course, I was stupid for saying yes to the scam anyhow. But at the end of the day, I wanted to be with Troy.

Dahlia, however, in the end hated us together, which started all the heartaches in our little circle.

Now looking at Troy, sitting in the driver's seat, gripping the steering wheel, made me think. I waited for him to say Teresa was lying but that did not come out of his mouth. Instead he sat across from me as if he were waiting for a reaction. Was this a show he was putting on for her sake, so that they could witness my pain? It was cruel being in the vicinity of the woman he had originally cheated on me with a while back. I still felt like a fool. Why her? A little over a year ago Troy and I were in love. Despite all the mess and the fact we both withheld secrets, we loved each other. He never knew why I started to date him. He never told me about his past with Dahlia, nor did he tell me about Teresa. We were doomed from the get-go. I had agreed to the scam, and I had different motives from the beginning. Troy also had secrets. He never wanted anyone to find out about Dahlia and he. But this wasn't what made us breakup the first time. When I had found out that he had possibly fathered a child by Dahlia's sister, I went livid. Fortunately, Troy wasn't the father but Dahlia's current boyfriend was, which was reason number one for me and Troy's reunion. Now, Dahlia was happy when we had broken up. But when she saw we had gotten back together, her hate for Troy had resurfaced, causing her to tell everyone about the scam, which in turn was the reason why Troy and I broke up for the last time. Until today, I hadn't spoken to him or seen him since our last goodbye a year ago.

Teresa was his other woman the whole time we had dated. I had given Troy my heat but he was never faithful to me until it was too late. I cleared my thoughts. No one had uttered a sound in the last few minutes. I didn't wish them well, so saying congratulations would be a lie.

I wanted Troy to marry me. I wanted to make love to him in the front seat of his truck right in front of her, just to show her who was boss. But I couldn't do that. I couldn't make a scene. My best friend's wedding reception was going on ten feet away from us. I had to stay calm.

"Married, well that is a surprise. I guess I should say congrats," I said to finally break the silence.

"Yeah, you can do that and get the hell out of my fiancé's car," Teresa said, her screeching voice threatening to drawn unwanted attention.

"Teresa, calm down. We are just talking. It's been awhile." Troy fixed her with a stern expression.

Who does this chick think she is? I fought to stay calm, refusing to give her the time of day. "You know what Troy, before you leave, I want to catch-up. You know where to find me." I hopped out of his truck.

Teresa rolled her eyes at me.

"Yeah I will be in town for a while, and I definitely know how to find you."

I walked away listening to Teresa cuss up a storm. I laughed inside at her as I realized that his departing statement was the proof I needed that it was not too late for us.

***

Jazz and Tim had really done the marriage thing. Everything around me was changing. I walked back to the reception area and spotted Dahlia sitting at a table alone eating cake. I told her everything that had just happened.

"You were in his car?" She stared at me with her mouth open.

"Yes, and he made some weird comments. I know he wants to talk more. I can feel it."

"After all this time, why now and why with Teresa here?"

Dahlia had a good point. Why finally talk to me after all these months. He knew he wasn't here alone and that at some point Teresa would be looking for him. Troy hadn't made an effort to contact me at all and I didn't understand why today of all days.

"I don't know why he chose now," I said. "I am just excited that I finally saw him."

Dahlia rolled her eyes at me. She would never like Troy and I couldn't blame her. After so many months of she and I not talking, we finally became close again after Jazz gave birth. I guess Jazz's bringing a child in the world made us let go of our pride and finally talk. For months we didn't communicate at all because she had told Troy about the scam. I felt as if she had betrayed me and therefore had lost my trust.

Dahlia told me how Troy had pulled a stunt on her in front of our classmates back in college. I couldn't imagine going through what she had, knowing that hundreds of folks saw her naked. Back in college Troy wanted to enter a fraternity and to do so, Dahlia was his designated target. He dated her and made it seem as though they were serious. He proposed to her as a part of the ploy and secretly recorded them having sex.

The night he was to be accepted into the fraternity, Troy played the tape in front of a hundred people, Dahlia included. From the night she watched her naked body on a television screen in front of a room full of people, she hadn't talked to Troy since. That was until she came up with the scam and had recruited me to do her dirty work. I was so surprised that I never knew. How had I not found out? I also never understood why Troy did what he had done and not become a part of the fraternity. He didn't seem that awful of a person after hearing that part. But Dahlia wouldn't forgive Troy. I figured what happened years ago prior to my relationship with Troy had nothing to do with me or who he was now.

I needed to get away, to go home and rest. The DJ played Tony Terry's *With You,* and I immediately started to feel the emptiness in my life.

"Why the hell are they playing that damn song now?" Dahlia said, her voice a quiet whisper.

The words to the song stabbed both of us in the heart. Karma!

I looked up and saw Robert, Troy's brother, the man Dahlia had dated and fell in love with a little over two years ago. He was walking our way. My heart began to flutter. "Dahlia, Robert is coming this way; he looks like he is going to ask you to dance." Her eyes widened and she almost choked on her piece of cake.

"What, where is he?"

"Right behind you," Robert said before I could.

He stood there tall and confident. His light skin was unbelievably attractive and smooth. Robert was just as handsome as Troy.

He extended his hand. "Come on, Dahlia, this is my song. Our song."

My eyes began to water with excitement for Dahlia. She slightly elbowed me in the arm before taking his hand. They whispered in each others ear like they used to months ago before their breakup. Robert never knew of Troy and Dahlia's past. So when it all came out, he broke it off with Dahlia and said that it was too much drama to digest.

I used to be happy that he had left her like Troy had left me. Now, however, I see that no one deserves to be alone, even if they had lied to gain trust. Dahlia glowed in Robert's presence. Her bridesmaids dress swayed as she graced the floor. She looked beautiful with him. I was jealous. Where was my prince charming? Wherever he was, he wasn't here.

Dahlia Jones

I'm Dahlia Jones, and the person who decided to start the scam in the first place. Some may ask why I didn't just get back at Troy by myself. That would have been too easy. I wanted him to suffer. The fact was his heart was broken and my planned worked. In the midst of that, Nitrah fell for him and her heart was broken, too. We'd lost our friendship for almost a year, and I lost the love of my life, Robert. Ironically, Robert is Troy's brother. I had no intentions of dating Robert but nature took its own course and I followed. I guess we all have our side of the story; I am not all bad as I seem.

I had no way of knowing that Robert was going to pop back into my life today. Why at Jazz's wedding of all places? It had been months since I'd last heard from Robert. When he left me last year, I couldn't blame him because of what I'd done and who I was. I imagined he felt like I was a bad person because I tried to hurt Troy the way I had been hurt. Robert also felt like I was not over Troy. The whole truth came out one night when we all were out at the Rhapsody Club. I blatantly blurted out the whole scam idea—losing Nitrah's friendship and Robert's trust in the process. My hate for Troy would probably never be resolved. I pretended like I'd moved on, but I hadn't.

After dancing with Robert, my pussy started to throb. Only Robert gave me that feeling. I quickly moved away from him. I needed separation before I gave in to my urges. I still craved him and I still had hopes for us. But I couldn't help but think that Robert only danced with me to be nice.

After running from Robert, I returned to the table to find that Nitrah had left. I couldn't blame her since everyone else in the room was happy except for us. We were the ones who were single and miserable. I walked out, jumped in my convertible, and let the top down so the wind could blow through my hair. I didn't say goodbye to the bride and groom or to my friends and family. I just drove off wishing I hadn't let my feelings for Robert resurface.

***

The next day I was late to class. I hated being back in school. After Robert and Nitrah had cut me off last year, I decided to go back and finish up with my masters degree. Life was better. I received an associate's position at Anderson Marketing Firm in Dallas and also purchased a house in Irving. It was a forty-five minute drive from Fort Worth, and it was worth the distance away from my social circle. My house was in an older suburb right in the middle of Dallas and Fort Worth. I had three bedrooms, a guest room, an ice, a living and dining area, and a gigantic backyard. I was finally doing well. Even Nitrah had changed somethings in her life. She was teaching middle school and regularly performing Spoken Word Poetry at open-ic night at Rhapsody. I supported her whenever I could. Sometimes I could tell that her poem was about me or Troy. Other times, though, I was certain that she was speaking about Denim.

Denim was Nitrah's ex, a truth that Jazz, Charmaine, and I all wanted to keep that way. He'd become a well-known DJ and moved to Houston where he produced music for Swisha House Records. Denim and Nitrah never spoke anymore. Denim had plenty of women due to his six-figure salary. He had one main thing about him: he was a cheater, and he always seemed to jump back into Nitrah's life when she was happy and had moved on. I figured she wrote poems about him because she missed their friendship. They had known each other for almost twenty years. When he moved on and had moved away it was like he never existed.

While sitting in class thinking about Nitrah, I glanced at my watch hoping we were almost finished. The long hours and demanding homework schedule was working my last nerve. I struggled to keep my eyes open because the teacher was boring. I still had to go to work, meaning today was going to be a long one.

***

Arriving at work, I parked my car in my new parking spot then headed toward the entrance. I grabbed a cup of morning coffee then headed towards the elevator.

"Excuse me, are you Dahlia Jones?" I heard someone say as soon as I entered the floor.

I turned around and saw a petite woman. She was a caramel-brown complexion with pretty, long hair extensions.

"Yes I am Dahlia, who are you?"

She extended her hand. "Oh, sorry, I'm Monica Daniels. I start today. Mr. Withers told me to connect with you on how to start my position."

"Oh, yes, he did tell me that." I looked at my watch. "You're early. Follow me into the office and I'll show you to your new desk." I proceeded to show Monica around. We had small talk as I showed her the ropes around the office.

Monica was starting as a secretary. I reviewed her résumé and noticed that she didn't have a degree of any kind. I wasn't sure how in the world she got this position, because even a secretary needs a bachelor's degree. I started to train her for her position. Since Monica was from Chicago, I showed her around Dallas after work and we had dinner at Johnny's Soul Food Restaurant. She was really cool and down to earth. I just knew that my girls would click with her instantly. She seemed like a person we could add to our circle of friends. That was what I thought when I first met her, but I had no idea of how deceptive her motives really were.

Nitrah Hill

A week after Jazz's wedding Troy kept his promise and called me. I agreed to meet him at the Sausage Joint, a barbecue spot in Fort Worth. I was nervous because he was sneaking away from Teresa to meet me. I had incorrectly assumed that he had gone back to San Antonio by now, so I was glad to hear that he was still in town and wanted to meet. When I drove up I saw his truck. I parked and got out. The aroma of barbecue sauce made my stomach growl. I decided that I wanted to order my favorite chopped beef sandwich.

Troy had beat me to it.

He was seated in the far back with a large sandwich and two slices of 7up cake.

"Are you trying to con me?" I eyed my favorite food on the table.

"Naw, I knew you would want your chopped beef. We could never drive down this street without you wanting to stop in for it."

"You sure are right." I sat down in front of the tray. I noticed his smile as I took a bite. I closed my eyes as I chewed, enjoying the sweet flavor. "So you got me here, what's up?"

"I wanted to tell you in person that I'll be coaching at North Trimble next semester."

"Are you? Congrats on that. Why did you need to tell me?"

"Don't really know why, but I do know that I wanted to see you. I had to see you."

I stared at him with a blank look. I didn't want to play anymore games with Troy. "Okay so you told me, congrats."

"I see you won't let this be easy?"

"What is this, Troy? What do you want to be easy?"

He leaned forward and placed his face in his palms, rubbing his temples. I took another bite of my sandwich and waited for his response.

"Nitrah, I am tired of this. We need to talk."

I wiped my mouth again. "Talk, Troy, go ahead. What do you have to say after all these months of no contact? That you are marrying her of all people? Her?" I laughed my disgust showing in the forced chuckle. My hand began to shake. My emotions were bubbling over.

He placed his hand on top of mine. "Nitrah, I am sorry for that. Teresa said that out of spite. She wants to get married, I just never told her no."

"You sat there and stared at me as if you wanted me to hurt from her statement. You didn't object at all."

"I know. I did that to hurt you. I'm sorry. It's just that I wanted you to hurt."

I snatched my hand away. "You wanted me to hurt? I have been hurting. It's been like a year since this shit about the scam came out. I have been hurting since then. You sit here and claim that I haven't been hurt. I have. You threw us away like it was nothing. No phone call or anything. You made love to me that night you told me you were moving to San Antonio. That morning you were gone. There were no calls from you. Not until the day of Jazz's wedding. Now tell me, am I not supposed to feel pain?"

He moved to my side of the table. After a quiet moment, during which I stared at the table, he lifted my head gently, caressing my cheeks with both hands. Troy just sat there looking at me for a moment. Then he kissed me, slowly placing his lips against mine.

I instantly felt a sexual rush across my body and pulled away. "I can't do this, Troy."

He dropped his hands in surrender. "Do what?"

"This thing. We go back and forth. You say you love me then disappear. I can't do this anymore."

"I know, Nitrah. In truth I am confused about what went down with us and why we are at odds."

"Troy, if you say that shit one more time, I swear. We are at odds because you left. You didn't get my side, you just left. How can we heal if you do things like that? I don't know anymore. I am tired of my heart loving you and being stomped on. I just don't know." I lowered my head.

"I know, I have to sort this thing out with Teresa and then we can hopefully start over."

I stood up. "Troy, do what you want to do, but I am no longer putting my life on hold." I walked out the door in hopes of a new beginning. I was tired of this merry-go-round. I hopped in my Jeep and sped off. Tears stung my eyes as they fell. I headed to Rhapsody, my favorite spot to relax.

***

It was early in the day so the club's crowd was light. I went to the top level and relaxed on the outside patio. They played Lalah Hathaway, her smooth vocals soothed my soul. I ordered some wine. Rhapsody was the perfect place to get away. Lately I'd become something of a celebrity at Rhapsody because I perform on open-mic nights. The audience accepted me with open arms and I loved it.

The wine eventually mellowed me out. Then I began hearing things.

Nitrah is that you?

I ignored the voice until someone tapped my shoulder. I jumped out of my trance, on the verge of yelling, when I spotted Michael. My breath escaped me. I couldn't believe it. I blinked twice to make sure I wasn't dreaming.

"Nitrah, hey, I knew that was you," Michael said.

I almost lost my balance when I jumped from my seat. "Michael. Michael Williams, am I seeing you right now?" That was a stupid question. I hadn't seen him in over a year.

He wrapped his arms around my waist and gave me a gentle hug. "Yeah, it's me, girl. How you been?"

He smelled so good. I hadn't thought about him in a while, not since we broke up over a year ago. He was Troy's former friend, a friend with whom I had a small affair. Although we never had sex, he used to treat me so good. He left a year ago to pursue an internship in Atlanta. We had a strong connection, but not so much that I thought I would ever see him again.

"Nice to see you too, girl. It's been awhile."

"I never thought I would see you again." I glanced around him to see if he was with someone else. I didn't see anyone. "What are you doing here?"

"I come here for lunch meetings. Just finished one and here you are." He had that daze in his eyes.

I recognized his sexual stare. I could recognize it in any man's eyes. I gave him the same look; it had been months since I had any. Then a red flag went up: I remembered that Troy was back in town. I looked at the floor. I didn't need anymore drama. "So you're back in Dallas now?"

"Been back now for about three months. I head a sports agency now and work with some of the players from the Mavericks. I think I met your brother. Jailen, right?"

"Yeah, he's a trainer for them. How did you connect me to him?"

"I remembered you mentioned it awhile back. His last name is Hill, so I put two and two together."

"You were always a good listener."

He directed me back down to my seat as he sat across from me. He looked the same, but somehow he had a smoother look now that he was a successful sports agent. *What a catch.*

"So what's new with you?" he said.

"Well, I teach at a middle school now and I kind of headline a Spoken Word Poetry show here twice a month. Other than that, same old same old."

He nodded. "I would be lying if I said I didn't know you did Spoken Word here. They have a nice flyer of you at the information desk."

"Oh, really, so you knew you could see me here?"

He hesitated for a moment. "Yes, Nitrah, I did. I have wanted to meet up with you for a while now."

My mouth went dry and I started to get the bubble guts. What was Michael implying? "You wanted to meet up with me?"

"We had unfinished business awhile back. I never stopped thinking about what could have happened."

"Oh, lord, what a day," the words slipped from my lips.

"I'm sorry. Am I wrong for saying this?"

"Oh no no, it's really sweet. It's just a shock. I haven't seen you in a while. I had released you and everything we had."

"Released me?"

"I accepted the fact that you were gone. I let it go to get past it. I knew you had to go but the fact that you are back is a little overwhelming."

"I never stopped thinking about you, Nitrah; I never expected to move back to Fort Worth this soon."

I started to relax and talking felt easier. I felt comfortable with him again, which confused me. Why did he come back now, just moments after Troy's lips were on mines?

Tim Meadows

May 2004

I had just gotten off work when I realized that Jazz, my wife, and I had to attend one of Dahlia's casual house parties, which were popular in our social circle. Jazz was obviously looking forward to it, probably looking forward to releasing the tension from school.

When we arrived at the party, our goal was to have all the fun we could. I kind of missed my boys being around but Bobby, Charmaine's husband, and I grew to be real cool. He and I would hang out with some guys from the construction site.

I still hung out with Robert but on rare occasions. Since Robert and Troy were brothers and I was still with Jazz, who was best friends with Nitrah, we seldom hung out to avoid talking about the drama that had gone down.

Robert told me a few weeks ago that Troy was coming back, which only meant one thing: I had to hear Jazz's mouth about him and Nitrah, which I was sure was going to happen. Jazz loved to gossip, and since we'd settled down and became a family, she has had less time to hang out, meaning things were about to change.

The party was rocking with its normal crowd. Dahlia lived in Irving, which was a nice suburb. I looked forward to the day I could get my family out of the townhouse we were living in.

Jazz went off to talk to her friends while I grabbed a beer. As I opened it, I accidentally bumped into a lady who I had never seen before. "Excuse me, miss."

"It's cool, don't worry about it." She proceeded to wipe off the beer that had splattered on her shirt.

"Damn, I am so sorry about that. I should have seen you coming."

"Like I said, it's cool. Dahlia has it pretty crowded in here anyways. I am Monica. You are?" She extended her hand to me.

"Tim, I am Jazz's husband." I hurried and let her hand go.

"Jazz. I haven't met her yet but Dahlia talks about her."

"How do you know Dahlia?"

"I work with her. I started last month at the firm. She's real cool people."

We stood there in an awkward silence for a few moments. I didn't want to let her walk away, but I couldn't think of anything to say. I looked at her round eyes and shapely lips. I probably needed to get away from her before I got caught up. "Well, it is nice to meet you then. Have fun."

"Thanks. Talk to you later."

I walked over to where Bobby and a few more of the guys were standing. "Hey guys, what are we playing tonight?"

"What's up, Tim? We're about to play some tonk and then some dominoes, so pull out a twenty and grab a spot." Bobby pounded his fist lightly against mine.

"That's what's up," I said and grabbed a seat.

"Yo, Tim, I saw you talking to Dahlia's new friend. What's her name?"

Lester said. He was a friend from work.

I tried to play it cool although I didn't want to share the information. "Don't remember."

"Damn, she is fine as hell. Is she single?" Lester almost showed his hand as he glanced back at me.

"Man, concentrate on the game," Bobby said.

Out of the corner of my eyes I saw Dahlia jump out of her seat just as Marvin Gaye's *Sexual Healing* played through the system. The living room furniture had been cleared out to create a dance-floor vibe, and other ladies were joining her as they swayed to the music.

My eyes sought out Jazz. I was curious to see if she would dance since she was always shy. As usual, she remained planted in her seat as she rocked to the music and laughed at her friends. Nitrah pulled at her, trying to force her to stand up and dance, but Jazz waved her off.

I felt like someone was watching me. I scanned the room slowly, wondering where the sensation was coming from. Out of the corner of my eye, I noticed Monica dancing. She stood there doing a sexy dance and staring right in my face.

It shook me a little.

I turned my head instantly like I had just seen something that I knew was forbidden. Then I felt like a chump. A grown man looking away from a sexy woman. Was I crazy? I turned back to see if I was mistaken, but there she was again staring at me with lustful eyes.

I glanced at the guys, but they were too busy playing cards. I looked in my wife's direction, but she was focused on her girls on the dance floor. I turned my head back toward Monica. She was smiling at me while shaking her hips in small circles. Excitement trickled through me.

"Yo, Tim. Man, it's your play. Come on."

Bobby's loud voice tore through my haze, snatching me from Monica's trance. "My bad." I glanced at my cards and turned my back to Monica. The realization that another woman had excited me in a room full of my friends, with my wife just inches from her, also shook me up. I was afraid of what I might do. I simply didn't trust myself.

Troy Washington

I went back to San Antonio and moved my things to my new spot in the Burleson area right next to Fort Worth. It had been a couple weeks since I had last talked to Nitrah, which was killing me because her last words cut me deep. I only hoped she hadn't given up on me. I know that being missing in action hadn't helped, but my pride got in the way.

I wanted to break- up with Teresa and pursue Nitrah before it was too late. Teresa was on my ass since she had saw me talking to Nitrah at Jazz and Tim's wedding. Teresa was continually questioning me and her routine was getting on my nerves. I was glad when Tim called me up and said he was taking me out to have some fun with the guys. I needed sometime away to just hang out.

I met up with them at Freddy's over in Woodhaven to play some pool, get drunk, and wild out. I flashed my ID at the bouncer as I strolled past. Tim and Robert stood at a pool table.

"Hey y'all. What we getting into tonight?"

"Aw hell y'all, it s about time this nigga made it back to funky town." Tim gave me a one hand shake.

I laughed. "Hell yeah, I had to get back and start taking over the city again."

"That's alright, bro, I took your spot." Robert laughed.

A man sitting on the high stool against the wall leaned forward and extended his hand. "Hey man, I'm Bobby."

"Bobby? Charmaine's husband, right?"

"Yeah, these two over here done went and got hitched." Robert gripped his beer.

I took off my jacket and threw it across a barstool. "Alright, somebody hand me a stick so I can show y'all how to hit it right."

We all laughed out. The night was going on well. I told them about my year in San Antonio; Tim told me about him and Jazz; Bobby talked about his job and Charmaine; and Robert talked about nothing really. Robert's dullness kind of surprised me. I didn't realize how boring my brother was, how his life wasn't growing or expanding into anything. We ended up playing three games of pool and then went to Jackson's Wings for a late-night meal.

Over food and beer, they finally decided to interrogate me about my relationships.

"So I saw Nitrah the other night," Tim said. "Oh yeah, and I saw Dahlia too. They sure are doing well without you two." He smirked.

"Man, why did you have to go there?" Bobby shoved Tim on the shoulder.

"Oh come on, you know I'm just messing with him. My bad, bro." Tim extended his fist and gave me a pound.

"Man, that Dahlia and Robert ship has sailed and docked," Robert said.

They all got quiet and looked at me. When I didn't respond, they all started shaking their head in disagreement.

"You still are going after her?" Tim said.

"I thought I missed all the drama, I guess not." Bobby shook his head.

"Bro, you aren't passed Nitrah yet?" Robert said.

"Look, if y'all must know, yeah I still got something for her, alright? Now shut up about it. Why are y'all trying to clown me?"

"Look, man, I'm just shocked that's all. Until my wedding, you didn't bother to see Nitrah. She done moved on, dated, switched jobs, and everything in between. Hell, I thought y'all were more than done," Tim said.

"Yeah I know. I have been taking my time with this."

"What are you planning on doing?" Robert said.

"I don't know yet."

Bobby added, "Well I don't know much about what happened over a year ago, but Char told me she just hooked back up with a dude named Michael."

Our table got quiet. My head dropped into my hands. "Bobby, please tell me you're not talking about Michael Williams." My voice was quiet.

"Mike? Where the hell he been at? He's with Nitrah now?" Robert said.

Tim threw up his hands. "Oh shit, Michael. Man, I'm sorry, Troy, I didn't know."

I looked at him with curious eyes. "What you mean?"

"Jazz mentioned something to me about it," Tim said. "I didn't pay any mind, and we supposed to go hear Nitrah speak at Rhapsody this weekend."

"Oh yeah, Char told me that too. I didn't know y'all have history with the guy," Bobby said.

"You mean to tell me that my former best friend and the woman I want are together?" They didn't answer; they just stared at me with apologetic eyes.

Robert said, "If it means anything, bro, I will go with you to Rhapsody this weekend."

"Hell yeah, I'm going to Rhapsody! I'm not only going, I'm going to perform."

"Perform?" Robert and Tim said in unison.

"Yeah, it's poetry night, right? It's time I showed Nitrah another side of me."

***

Robert and I arrived at the Rhapsody around 7:30 pm. As usual, we avoided the valet just in case we had to do a quick getaway. I sported jeans, my usual white tee, some Jordan's, and a round top hat. Robert was dressed similar but his shirt was black. I don't know why he chose to come with me to the club, but I was glad I wasn't alone. Neither Tim nor Bobby could ride along because they were with their women. I didn't ask Robert why he wasn't with Dahlia. It was a small relief because sometimes I hated to hear her name or see her face. She just reminded me of the past too much. The fact that she still holds a grudge didn't help either.

We parked Robert's Ford 1500 and headed for the main entrance. I was glad it was casual night or we wouldn't have been let in. I didn't see any familiar faces. Robert trailed behind me, leaving it up to me to spot the crowd I was searching for. I walked past the main lobby desk and saw a picture of Nitrah.

The photo cast the profile of her face. She looked beautiful. Her hair was straight and curled at the edges of her face. She didn't have on much makeup, her healthy dark skin glowed. I preferred her like this, natural and radiant. I kept my eyes on the picture, pretended that she was smiling at me.

"I think I see Nitrah," Robert said.

I followed the direction of his eyes. He was right, it was Nitrah. She was speaking with someone who worked at the club, and I could tell she was preparing to go on stage. Just in time, I thought. I walked over to the desk and placed my name on the list to speak.

"Come on, Robert, let's sit in the back." I was eager to see her perform because I had never heard her poetry.

She wore a nice fitted shirt and high shorts, almost like the boy shorts I used to love to see her in. Her hair was pinned up into a bun. I searched the crowd for the rest of the crew and that was when I saw Michael. He looked the same but he dressed better. It was obvious that he was holding a lot of money in the bank now. I envied seeing him sit in my spot. It made me sick to my stomach to think of him sleeping with Nitrah. Maybe I lucked up and they hadn't done anything yet. Maybe he would have to wait like I did. Then I remembered I probably had to wait because of the scam.

"Bro, are you alright?"

"Yeah I'm cool, just didn't want to see him that's all," I said, referring to Michael.

The crowd was packed upstairs and down. They played smooth jazz until a person went on the main stage to speak. My thoughts were interrupted when I heard Nitrah's voice.

"Where is he, the guy who signed in?"

I wondered who she was referring to. As I stared at her, she headed in my direction. It took a second before I realized that she was walking straight toward me.

"Troy, Nitrah is coming over here." Robert pointed her out to me. "Damn, man, what you gonna do? Are you scared now?" He teased.

I started to wish I hadn't brought him with me. I stood there and waited for Nitrah to reach me.

She had spotted me so I had to calm down. This was not the time to punk out.

"Troy, I saw you signed up to perform. What do you think you are doing?" She was angry. There was no indication that she was happy to see me and that kind of hurt.

"Yeah, I signed up. I got a few things to say."

"Are you trying to embarrass me? What is it that you want, dammit? Why must you be everywhere I am?"

I took her by her waist and said, "Come here. Just calm down, I ain't gonna bite." I guided her toward the top level of the club.

"Don't touch me, I can walk myself. You better explain to me why you are here." Her voice became intense.

We walked out onto the balcony, and I pretended that we were the only people out there. I wanted her to see a nice view while I said what was on my mind.

"I'm not here to hurt you, Nitrah. I'm here to just be close. Is that a bad thing?"

Her face was twisted in an expression of anger and confusion. "Be close to who?"

"To you, who else?"

A sarcastic chuckle forced itself from her mouth, but her lips didn't smile. "Whatever, Troy, I am out of patience with these games. As you can see I'm busy, and I'm no longer single."

That cut me deep. I coughed a little. It felt like my throat went dry. Was I to believe that Nitrah was serious about Michael? Or was she just dating him to make me jealous? I remembered when she last started up with him. After I had broken it off with her, she seemed to have no intentions to tell me she was dating him. So maybe—just like last time—she was serious about him and wasn't playing games. "What do you mean you are no longer single?"

"Just what I said. I'm sure you know by now. I'm tired of you walking in and out of my life. Who do you think you are? Yeah, maybe I brought the heartache on myself for doing that stupid scam, but it's been over a year, and I am not going to cry over you anymore. I just want—"

Is she with him just because I wasn't there? Just maybe I still have a chance.

I cut off her last words with a kiss. I needed the taste of her lips against mine. I kissed her with my most sincere passion. I knew she wouldn't fight it. There was no other man for her, she just hadn't figured it out yet.

Although I knew she wouldn't push me away, it rocked me that she kissed me back. Her kiss felt sincere and for a split moment, I felt she was back in my life loving only me.

When I opened my eyes she was looking at me. Her eyes were angry. I paused, surprised by the intensity pouring from her pupils. That was when she pushed me away. Surprise left me frozen. I stood there stupidly wondering what had just happened.

Nitrah wiped her lips with the back of her hand. "Troy, it's over. Just leave me alone."

The pain in her eyes was raw and deep. The hurt she had hidden all this time sat on the surface like a raw scar. The tears came all of a sudden and my heart wrenched. I would rather jump off the balcony than witness the turmoil I had caused her. The tables were turning on me. Yeah, I told her I was with Teresa, but I didn't care about her like that. But Nitrah being with Michael seemed real and I was afraid that I was not getting close to her but further away.

"Nitrah, I am not going to give up on us. I'm here now. Can't you see that? I love you and I want to be with you. Why are you with him and not me?"

Nitrah blinked at me, an incredulous expression spreading over her face. "I know he will never leave me like you did. I know he will not be standing in my face declaring his love while he is with another woman. Am I right? I mean you are still with Teresa, right?"

She had me there. I hadn't had the words to break it off with Teresa. I still had needs. Why should I give up convenience? I would eventually break it off with Teresa when the time was right. So maybe I hadn't changed as much as I thought.

"I'm trying, Nitrah, but you don't make it easy."

"I don't make it easy? Do you hear yourself? Troy, get it through your head, I'm tired and I'm done. Just leave me be."

"I am not going to give up on us, Nitrah. This here isn't done. You still love me, I still love you. We are going to be together, I just know it."

She let out a deep exhale. "Really? Is that what you think?"

"No, it's what I know. You know it too."

"I don't have time for this. I have to go." She pushed past me.

I could feel her internal struggle, her pride pushing her forward while her heart wanted her to stay with me. But she kept going.

I decided against speaking on the open mic tonight. Instead, I sat in the corner with Robert for a few more drinks, mulling over how to break up with Teresa. I was officially on the other end looking in. Nitrah had changed me, and I was starting to not like the weakness I had for her. As if I was forgetting who I truly was.

Tim Meadows

I must admit after marrying Jazz our life didn't get more exciting. Maybe we were stuck on making our family legal by getting married and giving our son a home. Of course we didn't plan on getting pregnant, but we fell in love so quick it felt like it was the right thing to do. Yes Jazz cooks, cleans, and takes care of home while going to school. But I guess I was getting tired of the routine.

Before I had met Jazz, Troy and I were considered the two dogs of the funk, a nickname for Fort Worth. In truth, we were enjoying women. We were both young and free with no obligations. But when Troy met Nitrah and I met Jazz, it seemed like our dog years went away. Mine left quicker than Troy's as I grew closer to Jazz and eventually moved her in with me. Our relationship felt so deep. After that we became pregnant and got married. Now that was the beginning of my supposed to be happily-ever-after. But I recently noticed that the dog in me was not completely buried.

I walked out to my car after work. It had been a long day of work and I knew Jazz was probably in a deep sleep. My stomach churned and reminded me that I needed to grab something to eat before I passed out from hunger. There was no place better then Taco Casa.

***

Ten minutes later I parked in Taco Casa's lot. I went in and ordered my favorite super nachos. I carried my tray to the dining area and found a seat in the corner. I closed my eyes to say grace, thankful for a chance to sit down and eat in quiet. When I opened my eyes, Monica was sitting at my table, a seductive grin on her face.

"Tim, right?"

I remembered her. I remembered the thrill her flirting had sent through me, awakening emotions that had been stifled for years. "Yes and you are?" I was irritated that she was bold enough to disturb my meal, bold enough to approach me like I was single.

"Monica, I'm Dahlia's friend from work. We met at her house gathering."

I nodded my head. "Right, Monica, I remember. What are you doing way out here?"

"Love the tacos," she said, nodding at her tray.

The slight nod of her head reminded me of the night at the house. I shook my head slightly.

"Are you alright?" She said.

"The food is a little spicy."

"That's why I come here, I love the spices. I always ask for extra on my burrito."

"Cool." I returned my eyes to my food. I wanted her to move on. I wanted to enjoy my food alone. Better yet, I needed to be away from temptation.

"And jalapeños work well on everything," she said.

She obviously didn't take a hint well. I didn't say anything.

"I just about burnt out all my taste buds." She giggled. Her smile was beautiful.

It was ironic that her name was Monica. She reminded me of the singer. She had a red rose tattooed on her left breast. I tried to avoid staring at her chest, but they swayed as she moved. There was something about her that felt sensual and erotic. She was obviously bad news for me. My pulse quickened as I kept my eyes down. I tried to look at my food but my eyes kept bouncing from the table to her breasts.

She made me feel like Jazz used to. What was happening to me?

She said, "Did you just get off work?"

"Yeah, I pulled a later shift than usual. But I had to get some tacos. "I feel ya. Dallas is supposed to be getting a Taco Casa, but until then, here I am." I raised my eyes and met her kind smile. Here she was. Monica held my attention. As a result, we ended up chatting for a couple of hours. She was easy to talk to. She talked about her life, about how she played basketball every weekend like I did. I tried to think of her as one of the guys. I tried to convince myself that she was a potential friend, a female homeboy. But my eyes kept returning to her rose.

Nitrah Hill

I had finally finished up my administration work and I was now off for the summer. This year in particular was hard on my job because my passion had trailed off to my poetry. Even though I had not let it mess with my teachings, I knew that this was my last year as a full-time teacher. I planned on speaking with the owner of Rhapsody about potential summer events for open mic. They had been very open to me because of the high attendance for the poetic nights. I was so looking forward to a more active role in the club during the summer. Walking out the back door of my school, I noticed a woman standing by my car. Her back was to me so I didn't realize who she was. She heard my footsteps and turned around.

"Teresa, what are you doing here?" I said.

"I needed to talk to you."

This bitch is about to go psycho on me. I hadn't had a brawl with a woman in several years and I wasn't about to start now. "Why are you at my job, what do you want?"

"I talked to Troy."

I rolled my eyes at the mention of his name. "And?"

"You still want him."

"Troy and I are done, Teresa. Isn't that obvious?"

"I want you to leave him alone."

I chuckled. "Teresa, I have no intentions of going back to Troy."

She walked up to me and stood mere inches away, nose to nose. "You better not or else I will have to kick your ass."

"If you don't get your stank ass out of my face." I smirked. "This shit you're talking right here doesn't even interest me. You are at my job and I am a heartbeat away from calling security on you for trespassing."

As if on cue, the security guard walked by and eyed Teresa as he spoke to me. "Miss Hill, is everything alright?"

"Oh yes, Joe, this trespasser was just leaving the premises."

"You will see me again," Teresa said, backing up.

"Bitch, please. No one wants Troy's cheating ass." I hopped into my Jeep and sped off.

Troy's and Teresa's bullshit was getting on my nerves, and the last thing I needed was Teresa playing *Fatal Attraction.* I was a little angry at myself for letting the younger Nitrah surface. I was too old for these games.

I was about to end this. I drove straight to his job to confront him once and for all. I parked my Jeep across the street of the school by the football field away from any students. I reached into my purse and pulled out my cell phone.

"Hello," Troy answered on the third ring.

"I need you to come outside. I'm by your football field, across the street at the gas station."

"You are?" He sounded excited.

I was annoyed. I was even more annoyed that it took more than ten minutes for him to come over. My car was running hot and my air conditioner was blowing stale air under the hot Texas sun. I climbed out of the car and leaned against it.

"Your girl Teresa has a fatal attraction going on."

He raised a brow. "What do you mean?"

"She threatened me at my job. What did you say to her?"

"Aw man." He stopped just in front of me. "For real? I am so sorry. I broke it off with her. I told her that I was in love with you."

I rolled my eyes at him. "Ugh!"

"Why do you do that?"

"Do what?"

"Roll your eyes when I say I love you. You don't believe me, huh?"

"What do you expect Troy, that I will believe it and fall head over heels in love with you again?"

"After all this time, after all that we've had, you still want to make this difficult."

"Oh my God." I threw my hands in the air. "Troy, you just have no idea how much I am tired of you and this situation."

"Tired of me? The Troyon Washington people used to know is long gone. Is that what you want me to be, like I used to be? If I can't be with you then who can I be with? No one is you."

"I can't do this. I'm with Michael now and he loves me."

Troy leaned in toward me as if he wanted to hit something or me. I jumped back, shocked at his reaction. *I shouldn't have mentioned his name.* I remembered the night he got physical with Denim a couple of years back but until today, I hadn't seen him so angry at me just from mentioning Michael's name. I could tell he was hurt. Maybe now he would get the point.

"Is that what you want, for me to hear about my former best friend with you? I'm not going to take too much of you telling me this shit."

"Or what, what are you going to do, Troy?" I challenged. I grew quiet. Did I want to be the one to break a man down? Yeah maybe I did because of how he allowed Teresa to confront me. I yelled, "Look, I'm with Michael believe it or not. Just like you wanted to move on, well I do too."

"Is this it, Nitrah? Is this really what you want?"

I didn't want to answer. I knew that whatever I said would be final. I couldn't take the words back once they were spoken. But I had to move on, Troy was risky and Michael was safe. "This is it, Troy. I'm sorry." I couldn't read his expression as I told him my final answer.

"Until now, I always thought that just maybe," he said in between pants." This is what you want!" He turned and walked away. He was furious.

"I am so sorry, Troy." My voice was loud and it cracked under my pain. Tears ran down my face. I opened my car door and placed my head on my steering wheel and cried until I finally found the strength to turn on the car and drive away.

Jazzaray Meadows

My mama offered to watch Junior for a day. I submerged myself in the salon, finally enjoying a manicure and a pedicure as well as a new look and a new color in my hair. I felt like a new woman.

It was exactly what I needed, some time alone to do whatever I wanted. School was kicking my butt, Junior was a twenty-four-seven job, and Tim was always tired when he got home. I enjoyed the married life but it always seemed as if I had to worry about everyone else's well-being instead of mine.

I floated on freedom's cloud right up until I stopped at my mailbox on my way back into the house. The normal bills and advertisements filled my arms. As I sifted through the envelopes, I came across an unfamiliar return address in Tarrant County. I opened the envelope as I climbed the steps to my front door, wondering which telemarketer had gotten our information.

The paper was headlined the State of Texas *vs.* Jazzaray Meadows. *What the hell is this?* I continued to read. I was being sued for three million dollars for the murder of Terrence Wills.

I dropped the paper as if it were on fire.

I couldn't believe it. Terrence's mother, Jane Wills, was pursuing a civil suit against me. My heart dropped and I began breathing heavily. The more I tried to catch my breath, the more difficult it became. Everything around me began to blur. I stumbled toward the front door, hoping to get to the phone for help. I wasn't going to make it. I was having a panic attack. My mind new it, but I couldn't stop it from happening. I was going to pass out. I turned the other direction, heading for the steps. I couldn't make out my steps and tripped and fell over something hard. I began crawling for dear life, trying to get to a phone. Someone had to help me.

"Miss, are you alright?"

The words were distant. I thought I was hallucinating. I heard the voice again. Someone was there. I tried to speak, to tell them that I was having an attack but nothing came out. My eyes rolled to the back of my head and I was back in Terrence's living room, back to the day when I had killed him.

"So who is the dude? Just tell me already," Terrence yelled.

"Do you really want to know?" I yelled back.

"Yeah, that dude messed up my damn eye. You sleeping with him and now he is trying to take you away from me."

"Terrence, honestly, we need to talk. Our relationship has been sour for a year. I'm tired of this on-and-off again crap."

"We have been working at it," Terrence said, standing up. He was already getting angry and I had not broken up with him yet.

"Hold up, Terrence! Why are you getting mad all of a sudden?"

"Bitch, you are trying to break up with me over that punk-ass dude?"

All of a sudden fear crawled all over my flesh. At that moment, I wished I had met him in public. I rose up quickly and ran to the door. I knew something was about to happen and I needed to get away.

Terrence grabbed me by the arm and yelled, "Where the hell are you going?"

"Tim, you're acting crazy right now."

His eyes got so huge, all I saw was evil. I did not see the Terrence I once knew.

When he screamed, "Tim!" I realized I had just called him by the wrong name.

"Terrence, just let me go. Let's just talk."

"Bitch, you're fucking him, aren't you?" He shook me by my arms.

I screamed back, "You're fucking somebody else yourself."

Terrence slammed me across the couch. I fell back trying to catch my breath. Then the unthinkable was about to happen. He was about to rape me in his own home.

"Get off me!" I screamed at him, kicking and scratching with all my strength. All the while he was holding me down and trying to pry my legs open. Then there was a big bang on his front door.

Terrence turned around and yelled, "Shit!" He knew someone had heard us. He released one of my hands long enough for me to get my knife off my key chain. Someone kept banging on his front door.

Terrence turned to me and said, "Say one thing and I'm going to kick your ass."

"Fuck you! Help, someone come and help me!"

The knocks on the door became more rapid.

Terrance turned to me and said, "Bitch, I am going to fuck you up." Then he punched me twice in my face, causing me to fall back onto the couch. The room was spinning and I was in a daze, but I remembered my knife. I took my keys and jammed my key knife into his chest. He screamed out and collapsed on top of me. I pushed him off and tumbled to the floor, unable to catch my balance but desperately trying to get the hell out of there. I watched him roll over onto the floor. I struggled to my feet and started to run for the door before I realized my car keys were in his chest. I turned around and Terrence was not moving.

***

"Jazz." Someone's hand brushed across my head. "Jazz, can you hear me?"

My mouth felt dry. I tried to open my eyes. I was in a hospital room. Tim stood beside me. I looked over and saw Nitrah on the other end.

"Jazz, what happened, baby, are you okay?" Tim's eyes held the same look of fear I had seen in them before when I had multiple accidents like this soon after Terrence died.

My head ached. I must have hit it against the pavement when I passed out. "I. I don't know—"

"No, don't speak, Jazz. Take it slow," Nitrah said, grabbing my hand.

"It happened again, I'm sorry," I said as I started to cry.

Tim tried to quiet me, cradling me as if I were Junior.

"They are coming after me again, Tim. I knew they wouldn't leave me alone." The shock came to me suddenly; the memory of the letter brought back my fear in waves.

"Who, Jazz, who are you talking about? What happened today?" Nitrah held my hand tighter.

"Jane, she will not leave me alone."

"Jane?" Nitrah was confused.

I could tell Tim was replaying the name in his head. I knew when he realized who I was talking about. I saw it in his eyes.

"What does she want now? Did she call you?" Tim said.

"No, she had the county send me a letter for a civil suit."

"Civil suit, like for money? Who is Jane?" Nitrah was trying to understand.

Tim looked up at Nitrah and his expression silenced her.

"Jane Wills, Terrence's mother."

Nitrah's eyes said she understood, and then she started to look back at me.

"For murder. She is suing me for mental anguish because she claims I murdered Terrence."

"Murder!" Nitrah's voice bounced around the tiny room.

"How much is she suing for?" Tim became agitated.

I didn't want to tell him. I didn't know what would become of our lives now. What Jane was asking for was impossible.

"Jazz, did you hear me, how much is she asking for?" Tim sounded angry.

"Three million."

Nitrah released my hand and leaned back in her seat. Her eyes started to water. I looked at Tim.

"Three million! Shit, that's crazy. Why don't they leave us alone? That man attacked you. You were the victim. They allowed Jane to take this to court? We got to relive this over again?"

Nitrah came back closer to the bed. "Don't worry, this won't stand. I know a great lawyer who has handled civil cases before."

She held both our hands at the same time. I wanted to believe her, but I knew that it wasn't going to be that easy. We had no money.

"I can get Michael to help," she added.

Tim rolled his eyes at the mention of Michael's name. I guess he didn't like Michael now because of the rift it caused between the guys.

"Nitrah, I don't want anybody knowing about this. Not even Michael. Not yet." I stared at her.

"Why don't we just go see Jane and see if we can talk this thing out?" Tim folded his arms across his chest.

"No, Tim, not until we speak to a lawyer. Don't go do anything that could make it worst," Nitrah said. "Jazz, you know I got your back. Don't worry about this, okay?" Nitrah glanced at me with concern before she left the room.

I shook my head, looking more confident than what I actually felt.

***

I had been home for a couple of days. I kept remembering the day Terrence had died. It replayed over in my head like a DVD on repeat. I thought it was over. I thought I could live now. It was obvious that no matter what the police told Terrence's family about the day he died, they refused to believe that I was the victim. It had returned to haunt my house again. Now here it was again, right in my face. I tried to think of other things but Terrence always came back to my mind as if he were haunting my thoughts.

"Jazz, can you hear me?" Tim said.

"I'm sorry, what did you say?"

"I called you several times. Your mind is on this thing, huh?" He sat down and placed his hands around my waist.

I immediately felt uncomfortable. I scooted over away from his touch. "I was just thinking that's all." My reaction to his touch embarrassed me.

"Jazz, talk to me. What's wrong? You won't even let me touch you."

"I'm just a little tired. I have a lot of school work, and I have to go get Junior."

"Junior is fine. How about we go out tonight? It's the weekend, Nitrah called and said they were all heading out tonight, you should go. I think it would be good for you to get out of the house."

"I don't feel like it."

Rubbing his temples, he said, "Jazz, I'm tired of you sulking in this mess."

"What, Tim? What are you complaining about now? You are getting on my nerves."

"Do you think I'm going to allow you to fall into another depression? We went through this already, Jazz. This is how it started."

"Look, I'm just tired. I'm not thinking about that."

"The hell you're not. I know you. The last time they started to harass us you did this same routine. You know those folks got a large life insurance payment when Terrence died and all they do is harass us. I'm going to sue them."

"Sue them?"

"Yeah, I'm going to sue them for harassment. Look at all the times you been in the hospital. You were fine before this."

"I'm fine now." I sighed.

"You know that's a lie, but you keep saying it, hoping to make it true. We can't let them ruin us. Come on. Get up and let's go."

"I don't feel like it."

Tim observed me for a long time before he walked out the room. I heard the rear bedroom door close. I lay on the couch and cried. It wasn't always like this. I wasn't like this. I used to know happiness before I killed Terrence.

Nitrah Hill

June 2004

Michael was spending the day at my house. We had spent so much time together in the past few weeks. It felt weird to experience these emotions again. I felt like I was truly head over heels for this guy.

Tonight he offered to come to my house and cook dinner. He showered me with gifts and attention. He had my table filled with food; candles were lit all over my house; and rose petals were thrown on my hardwood floors and they led to my bedroom.

Butterflies fluttered in my stomach, and I knew what that meant. I hadn't had sex with him yet because when I looked at him, I thought about my argument with Troy at his job. I dreamt about that day over and over again. It played in my head like a bad video that wouldn't shut off. I hadn't seen Troy or spoken to him since our meeting by the football field. I knew that whatever he and I had was forever gone. *I got what I wished for.*

"Hey baby," Michael said, placing his arms around my waist and leading me to the dinning room table. "Welcome home."

"Hey yourself. Hmm, what do we have here?" I looked over the food.

"Mama taught me best."

I sat down in front of my plate and my mouth began to water. "I didn't know you could cook like this. I am never going to the kitchen again." I joked.

He laughed and said, "Go ahead and take a bite."

I was done eating in ten minutes. I was a little embarrassed at how greedily I ate. He didn't seem to notice, though, so I didn't say anything.

"I got that latest Will Downing CD today. Do you want me to put it in?" Michael headed for my system.

Did he just say put it in? Lord, doesn't this man know I'm horny as hell and here he goes using words like that. He's lucky I didn't jump across this table and tackle him in full-force mode.

"Baby, did you hear me?"

"Yeah, that's fine." I tried to minimize the thought of him rolling slowly in and out of me. I watched him walk across the room.

His ass was so damn perfect. He was teasing me with his swagger, he knew I was watching him.

I can't take this anymore. I need to release some pressure. I stood up as he put in the CD.

He turned and noticed me walking toward the back of the house. "Hey, where are you going?"

I stopped like a thief caught red-handed. I turned slowly and seductively said, "Come and find out." I know I don't have x-ray vision, but his bulge was calling me from his pants..

Now he was the one sexually excited. "You want me to follow you, huh? Where are we going?"

He was close enough for my hand to brush across his. I didn't want to wait anymore. He looked directly in my eyes and nodded in agreement. It was on. We were about to take our relationship to the next level. He walked into my room. The rose petals stopped at my bedroom door. I had expected them to be thrown across my bed.

"You didn't come into my room?"

"I have never been invited in so, no, I did not cross the threshold."

I smiled at him, loving everything about him. Michael was refreshingly handsome from his freshly shaven face to his masculine body to his soft hands. I wanted him to connect with me on a level so high that I could just float away.

"I want this to be about you." His voice was a tight whisper, tension mounting with each word.

I followed his orders and walked over to my bed. I sat and let my shoes fall off my feet. I felt nervous because Michael was different and special.

Michael removed his clothes, returning to me in blue boxers.

"Are you going to help me take this off?" I said, tugging at my shirt.

He licked his lips and said, "You know I am."

I lay back as he stood beside the bed and admired me. He slowly brushed his hands over my thigh, slightly up my skirt, and brought his hands to my blouse. I got dangerously wet. The look in his eyes was so genuine.

"I have been waiting for this day for two years," Michael said.

My heart anxiously pounded in my chest as he bent down to kiss my lips. He devoured my mouth, slowly caressing my tongue with his. He leaned beside me, placing his hands on the small of my back, caressing and rubbing. Lord, I was about to explode. I felt my clit stiffen with excitement as he nibbled on it with his teeth. *How did he get down there so fast?*

"Hmm, you taste so good." His words sounded muffled between sucks and licks and damn near eating a second feast.

I scooted my ass down farther toward his mouth. I wanted all of his tongue inside of me. "I want you inside of me, top drawer—grab that jacket!" I screamed out the words, trembling from my orgasm.

He jumped out of the bed and released his boxers from his body. My eyes jumped out of my head when I saw how big he was. He applied the protection and came back over to me.

"Are you ready for this?" he said.

"Yes, I am. Gently, okay?"

He did just that. I don't know how long he and I made love but by the time we were done, I felt bow-legged and sore. We lay in the bed, ate junk food, and had sex until the next day. I was falling hard for Michael.

***

Tonight the ladies and I wanted to go out. I needed to get Jazz out of her funk and I wanted to mellow out after being with Michael all week. I called Charmaine to see if she was ready.

"Hey Nitrah, what's up?"

"I'm calling to see if Bobby is going to let you out tonight." I laughed.

"I see you got jokes. Girl, please, he is going out with the guys tonight. So I am all good."

"Yeah, I see. You talk to Dahlia today? Homegirl is missing in action."

"Maybe yesterday, she has been with Joyclyn a lot, taking her everywhere, babysitting Darius, and all that other mess. Girl, I tell you Dahlia might as well have had the baby."

"Why is she taking care of Eric's kid like that anyways? Ugh. Joyclyn works my nerves, she know Dahlia's weak when it comes to her."

"Girl, I know. But she did tell me the other day she was going out with us, so before I leave I'm going to give her a call. The person we need to worry about is Jazzaray. Lord, I tell you, you all are going to run me into an early grave."

I rolled my eyes at the phone when I heard Charmaine acting like the mama again. I can remember sometime around Thanksgiving a couple years ago when Joyclyn's secrets came out. She was Dahlia's baby sister, the one who claimed to be pregnant by Troy but it turned out to be Eric's kid, who was Dahlia's boyfriend at the time. Till this day I cannot stand Joyclyn because she is bad news and lurks after men who are taken. Trying to get her off the phone, I said, "Okay, I will see you at the Sankofa Lounge. I'll go and get Jazz, don't worry about her."

***

I got into my car, drove off, and was at Jazz's door in less than thirty minutes. "Jazz, open the door. Now. I will use my key if you don't," I said in between knocks.

"Alright, girl, hold on." She opened the door and I saw that she was dressed, but she surely wasn't the glamorous Jazz I used to know.

"Are you wearing that?"

"Yeah, why?"

"Nothing, are you ready? I want to meet the girls on time."

"Alright, stop rushing me."

I noticed that her attitude and her demeanor seemed ugly and rude. She was a totally different person. *Maybe this night out will do her some good.*

***

When we finally arrived, I saw Charmaine reserving a table for us. She and Dahlia were talking to each other as they waited.

"Hey ladies," I yelled out in excitement.

"Ugh, why is everyone so dressed up?" Jazz complained.

All of our eyes were instantly on her as we noticed yet again she had an attitude. Homegirl was changing and for the worse.

"Hi to you too, Jazz," Dahlia said, standing up from the table and reaching out for a hug. Jazz gave her one but of course it wasn't sensual.

"So what is going on tonight?" I said, referring to the club's usual weekly themes.

"Oh, the Sankofa brought back Joel, that neo-soul artist we saw last spring,"

Charmaine said.

"Oh yeah, he was hot. I'm ready for a good time tonight, y'all. Michael has worked me out this past week."

Their faces lit up.

Dahlia said, "Oh really, just how much working out?"

"Well, let's just say I had to teach myself how to walk again."

We all burst out into laughs.

Jazz looked up behind me and said, "Well well well, isn't this going to be an interesting night."

We all turned to her with the same expression. She was putting a damper on the mood.

"Jazz, what is it now?" Charmaine was annoyed as were Dahlia and I.

"Oh I'm not trying to interrupt y'all. I just wanted to give Nitrah a heads-up."

"A heads-up on what?" Charmaine said.

Jazz tilted her head toward me and said, "Your boy Troy is here and he is not alone."

I looked back as if electricity had just shocked me, and I had a natural reaction. She wasn't lying, he was here. He looked happy but he also wasn't alone. He looked very happy with her. That's when I recognized who she was. Why her of all people?

"Is that who I think it is?" Charmaine said.

I think Dahlia giggled when she said, "Yeah, that's her. Miss Fiancée."

"I thought he broke up with her," Jazz said.

"Well I guess he lied about that too, or maybe they got back together. Who knows? Why on my first night out in a long time do I have to see him?"

"I saw him last week, but Teresa wasn't on his arm like tonight. So it looks like the old Troy is back to juggling more than one woman," Dahlia said.

"You saw him last week?" I said, looking at her directly in her face. I hated discussing Troy with her.

Dahlia frowned. "Yeah, isn't he old news? I don't have to tell you when I see him, do I?"

"Aw man, he just spotted me," Jazz whispered as if Troy could hear her.

Not wanting to turn back around and look at him, I looked straight ahead. "Stop looking over there then. Now he is going to know I know he is over there."

"Oh come on, just chill out. Oh shoot, never mind, he's walking this way," Charmaine said.

"He is, ah man. Why is he walking over here?" I whispered.

"Great, just what I need before I eat," Dahlia said in disgust.

"Nitrah!" I heard Troy say.

I turned around and put on a fake smile. "Troy."

He noticed my quick hello. He got the picture fairly quick.

"Well, I saw you all over here and I didn't want to be rude, so how are you all doing?"

"Fine," everyone said except for Dahlia.

At that moment I felt why she hated him so much.

"Well, you ladies, have a good night." He walked away as easily as he had come over.

I was a little disappointed. I expected him to want to pull me over to the side and for him to beg for my forgiveness yet again. But he didn't. He just walked away that easily. That walk must be getting easier for him. I realized then that his journey for me was over. So why did I all of a sudden feel bad and a need for him?

"Whew, now that's how I like it, a quick hello," Charmaine said.

"I agree," Dahlia chimed in.

I had to pretend I agreed so I nodded my head in agreement. The subject of Troy died fairly quickly as the night grew older. Joel was singing that tune I loved to hear to soothe my soul. The ladies and I decided to head to the balcony to listen in better and be able to see the entire stage.

I leaned my body up against the rail with my eyes closed, my face pointed toward the sky as I allowed Joel to sing to my soul. I found myself listening to his words and getting emotional. I opened my eyes remembering I wasn't alone. I didn't want my girls to see me cry. I didn't know why I was crying. But I remembered instantly when I looked over the balcony and my eyes locked with Troy's.

He was watching me, taking in the sight of my emotions. He was reading me as if he knew the story by heart. For a while we stood there with our eyes connected, not saying one thing to the people we were with. My girls didn't notice and Teresa didn't notice Troy either. It was as if we spoke a conversation but no words were spoken. All of a sudden the air left my lungs. I gasped and knelt down to the floor.

"Nitrah, are you alright?" someone asked me.

I played it off. "Oh, girl, it's just hot and I went out of breath in here. You know how I am." I stood back up to look down and saw Troy's face covered with concern. "Look, I'm going to head outside for a few minutes to get some air."

"Are you sure you're alright?" Jazz asked now concerned.

"Yeah," I yelled out as I started to walk toward the back to go downstairs. *Did seeing Troy do this to me? What is wrong with me? Get over him already.* I bumped into people who were rushing out the door. I ran down the sidewalk so fast I didn't hear anyone call my name. I was grabbed from behind and my defenses went up. I started to pull and yanked my arms to free myself of the strong grip.

"It's me, Troy!"

I finally calmed down enough to realize that it was him. I waved off the people around us who seemed to have taken concern.

"Nitrah, what's wrong? Are you alright?"

I couldn't answer him. I didn't know what was wrong with me. I knew I was emotional. But from what, I didn't know.

He grabbed my face with his hands, forcing me to look him directly in his eyes. "Nitrah, what's wrong? Talk to me."

He was concerned. I saw it in his eyes, in his demeanor, heard it in the tone of his voice.

"I don't know what's wrong with me." I gave up the fight and allowed myself to look at him.

He was angry and concerned all in one. He let go of my face and allowed his hands to drop to his side.

"You ran after me?" I said.

"Yeah."

"Why?"

"I don't know, natural reaction I guess."

"I'm sorry," I said.

"For what?"

"I couldn't get it out of my head."

He stood there waiting for me to continue.

"The last time I saw you. When I sleep, you haunt my dreams. That day just will not get out of my head." I was pulling at my head as if the memory was sitting on it and I wanted to take it off.

Troy took my hands and held them in his. My heart started to beat faster with his touch. *I thought I was over you.* I wanted to say that out loud but I couldn't. I could not let him know how I felt. Would he forgive me? Would he be angry, or would he just walk away now and leave me to cry?

"Nitrah, it's okay. I'm okay. I mean, what's done is done."

I shook my head as if I was answering a question and saying no.

"What can we say? We agreed to move on, right," he said. "I took it hard but what else can I do?"

"You can stay like this. You can stand here and tell me it's going to be alright. That we can get through this. That something is going to change."

"Change, like how?"

I whispered, "I thought I was over you." I titled my head, ashamed to look him in his eyes.

He released my hands slowly. "What do you mean?"

What am I doing? I should stop. I looked up, now bold enough to just risk it. I stepped toward him nearly quivering from nervousness. He stood there and watched me. He didn't move back. I saw him breathe in deep.

He whispered, "Nitrah I—"

"I know, Troy, but what do you want me to say, that I'm sorry? That I'm confused? I'm all of the above."

I saw he was resistant. As if everything went into slow motion, he raised his hands toward me. His fingers trailed across my arms, up my shoulders, and across my neck. As if he ran toward me and greedily took my lips to his, he started to kiss me. He kissed me hard, rough, and with so much passion tears poured down my eyes as I allowed him to explore my lips.

I wanted him to remember our taste, our connection, our history. He took his hands and pressed my body up against his. I could hear car horns blowing at us as they drove by. Some people were even cheering for our reconnection.

In between kisses Troy said, "I missed you. I don't know what were doing. We should stop but I can't. I want you. I need you."

I couldn't get one word in as he welcomed his lips on every corner of mines.

"Okay wait." I managed to say.

He pulled back, breathing heavily as if he had just run the marathon.

"Troy wait, we got to think about what were doing. I don't want to hurt anyone else."

"Okay, what do you want to do?"

"I don't know. I—"

"Don't do this to me again, Nitrah. Please don't make me regret this night."

"It's not that … well, it is kind of. I didn't expect to see you so soon, and now I am standing here kissing you knowing my friends could walk out and see us."

"So what if they did?" He was angry.

I tried to choose my words wisely, not wanting to repeat last month.

"You know I don't want to hurt anyone."

"Yeah, it seems like everyone but me."

"No, don't say that. Look, this isn't easy for me. We have rarely been together for like a year. It has been nothing but back and forth with us. I'm tired, and we need to make this transition easy and final."

"Okay, fine. What do you want me to do?"

"Wait."

"Wait on what?"

"For me to tell him."

"Who is he?"

I swallowed hard as I prepared to say his name. "Michael, you know I'm with him now."

"Here we go with this shit again." He backed up. "Call me when you're ready."

I grabbed his shirt. "Wait, don't do that. Just hear me out. I think I may love you both and I got to be careful how I do this."

He angrily pulled his arm away from me. "You fucking with me, right? You love him? Come on, Nitrah, damn. Why are you doing this to me? Was what I did so bad that you have to keep doing this to me? Huh! What the fuck do you want from me?"

"Wait, Troy, I know I am sorry. I tried to move on. Look, I'm going to make it right. I promise."

He was walking backwards away from me. "Why did I have to see you tonight? Why did I even run behind you?"

"I'm going to make this right, Troy. I promise you. I am not going to hurt us anymore!"

"You do what you want. I got to find someone who wants what I want."

I grabbed his hand and made him stand still. Now I was the one forcing him to look me in the face.

"Wait on me, Troy. I am going to make this right."

"This time, Nitrah, are we going to get this right?"

"I promise this is going to finally go in our favor. I love you, but I just got to tell him first."

Tim Meadows

July 2004

I answered my phone on the third ring. “Hey.”

“Hey, are we going out tonight?” Her voice tinkled in my ear and my heart rate quickened.

“Um, yeah, let me see what I can do. I got to get away first.”

“Is she home?”

“Yeah, and my son, so give me a minute and I will be right over.”

“Good. And bring some tacos, too.”

“Alright.” I hung up my cell and prepared myself for yet another lie. This time I was going to say I was headed to the gym. These days Jazz didn’t care anyway. We rarely spoke and since the lawsuit moved forward, neither one of us had been in the mood to do anything together. So I found me a hobby to occupy my mind.

I walked into our bedroom. Jazz had Junior cuddled up against her in a deep sleep. I stood there watching my family, trying to remember the last time when we were happy. I think that Jazz purposely pushed me away. As much as I tried to help her through this hard time, she wouldn't even let me touch her. Money was tight and all I ever wanted to do was leave the house to avoid an argument.

"Hey, Jazz, I am headed to the gym. I'll see you in a couple hours."

"Whatever. Lock the door on your way out," she said as I turned and walked away.

Getting out the house was easy but the guilt was growing stronger as I craved for my double life.

***

I pulled up in front of her house just in time for our favorite show to come on. That was what we did. We hung out, talked, and were there for each other. I walked up to the door and knocked.

"Hey Tim, you finally got here. I sure am hungry." Monica grabbed the tacos out of my hand and jumped on the couch. She made sure there was enough room for me to sit next to her.

"Yeah, I almost forgot you wanted them. Had to turn around. So what are we into tonight?"

"Well, you know the reruns of *Martin* are coming on and then it's whatever. I'm off work tomorrow, so I can stay up late."

I kicked my shoes off and placed them beside the couch to get more comfortable. "Did you get anymore beer this week? You ran out last time."

"Yep, grabbed some yesterday." Monica moved quickly, grabbing plates out of the cabinet and a beer from the refrigerator. "I hoped you would be by today." She reached into the freezer and pulled out a frosted glass, which she sat on a coaster in front of me on the wide coffee table. "See, always thinking about you."

I smiled.

She leaned over, placing the tacos on the plates. She put my plate on a tablecloth and sat it next to my beer. She leaned over and kissed me softly on the cheek. "How was your week?"

"It was hard work as usual. Nothing new. We got some new guys because we're behind on the construction site. But we look to pick up in the next two weeks.

"I hear you. Dahlia has me working so hard these days that I had to take a day off. Oh I got an idea. Why don't you take off tomorrow, too? We can just hang out here, you know."

"Take off work? Wow! I haven't actually done that since Junior was born."

"Then it's settled: you call in and we can hang out. Go to the water gardens or something. I haven't gone there since I moved here."

"I guess I can do that." *Jazz damn sure won't notice.* I wondered why Jazz couldn't be more like Monica. It just seemed easier to be around Monica, and now I was having doubts about my marriage. I knew I was probably feeling this way because of the lawsuit but something had to give. I looked over at Monica and started to realize how beautiful and attractive she was. How she was available at a time when I needed someone the most? I decided to just let everything go and let my and Monica's relationship flow. I was tired of being unhappy. Maybe this was the right direction for me.

"Hey, what are you over there thinking about?" She looked at me from the corner of her eye.

"Nothing."

"Come on, I can see it all over your face. What's wrong?" She leaned over and placed her hand on my knee.

I had to move her hand away because I became aroused by her touch. "I was just thinking how hard it's been at home and how easy it is with you."

"I'm sure you will find whatever you're looking for. This is a rough time. Don't let it take over you. I'm sure you used to laugh and be happy at some point. But I must say, I'm tired of looking at you being pitiful."

"Yeah, tell me about it. I understand what Jazz is going through, but sometimes I wonder am I supposed to go through it with her. Am I a bad husband to even feel that way?"

She scooted closer to me, eliminating the space between us. "You are a good man, Tim. I just know you will find what you're looking for."

I looked in her eyes. They were big, beautiful, and hazel. My heart started to race as I continued to stare at her. I knew what I was about to say would change the definition of our relationship. "What if what I was looking for was here?"

"Here, like here?" Monica said, pointing to the floor.

"Here, like with you." I put my hand on her leg.

She studied me. I guess she wanted to see if I was going to say anything else.

"I am not sure you mean what you say, Tim. I could be an easy way out."

"Look at us, we are practically together anyway, and I want to make sure that this is what I need to do."

"How do you plan on doing that?"

"I want to kiss you."

"You are really being bold. I don't know what to say. I don't think we should go there. I mean I like you, but I can cope with the fact that I got to you late. You're with Jazz."

I leaned in closer. I wanted some comfort. I needed Monica to be the one to help me heal, to make all this pain and frustration go away. "This could have been what was meant to be."

She exhaled, leaned back against her couch, and said, "I'm confused. I don't want to get hurt."

"I have never seen the rest of your house."

"Where in particular do you want to see?"

"Where do you sleep? I think we can get to know each other a lot more there."

"Where I sleep?"

I could tell she was trying to understand my message. She stood up and reached her hand out to me and said, "I have a king-sized bed. That's where I sleep."

***

Monica's room was dark but enough light shined through her blinds for me to see her bed. I wrapped my arms around her waist and brought her ass to my groin. I playfully brushed my hands across her ample breasts, while kissing her on the neck. She smelled like fruit and I opened my mouth to taste her. She moaned in acceptance. I turned her body around as I raised up her shirt tracing my fingers across her abdomen.

"Lay down," I said.

As she leaned back, I brought her shirt over her head. Her breasts stood at attention. I brought my mouth to them, sucking and tasting her nipples. I leaned up and pulled my shirt off as Monica rubbed my chest, smiling at my biceps. I placed my hands between her legs and, finding her wet pussy, I placed my fingers inside her. I could feel her clit stiffen as I twirled it with my thumb. Monica moaned as I continued to suck her breasts tracing my tongue from her navel to her neck. I pulled down her pants.

"Turn over. On your stomach."

She obeyed and I spread her legs like eagle wings and guided myself inside. I made sure she felt the depth of my dick in her pussy as I gyrated harder and faster. I made her ass slap against my groin as she screamed out in acceptance. I played with her clit to make her pussy crave more. I thrust inside her deep and rough. With each pound I loved the way I felt inside Monica. My mind was in a daze as I enjoyed the feeling of her pussy wrapped around my dick. I made sure I stayed deep inside her the entire night, not making it home until the next day.

Nitrah Hill

I had finally found a building I felt was reasonable. It was large with two floors, two offices, and a center stage. It was perfect. Michael helped me find it, and I was ready to put this into stone. I wanted this place to be mine. It was a nice building sitting by itself in a good part of Fort Worth. I would be the only poetic café in the city. I knew this was going to be a dream come true.

"Babe, what do you think?" Michael yelled out from upstairs.

"Besides some spring cleaning, this spot is perfect. We can add a patio outside for the spring and summer weather. Oh, baby, my spot is going to be hot."

"You damn right because my Nini is going to be running the joint."

For about a month now Michael had been calling me Nini, my new nickname. "So what are you going to call it?" he said.

"I don't know yet. I'm still a little clueless about the name. But I got the vision down pat. Also Rhapsody is going to help spread the word. I am so excited." I jumped into Michael's arms, embracing him with kisses and hugs.

"So when do you want to start working on it?"

"Shoot, I don't know. I'm going to be busy, I can tell you that. I know I'm still going to have to work. Maybe I'll substitute."

"Let's worry about that later. Let's go to the lawyer's office and sign the papers."

We hopped in his new Range Rover and drove over to his lawyer's office. I signed the papers. I was now the owner of my own club. I was more than excited, I felt ecstatic.

***

Dinner with the girls was something we tried to do once a month. Charmaine was now the director at the social security office; Jazz was focused on school more than ever; Dahlia was Miss Corporate World; and I was planning the big opening of Fort Worth's only poetic club. We tried a new Jamaican Cuisine spot that had recently opened up. This time around it didn't seem as if we were in a rush to leave. I was also more than curious to see what they were up to.

"I met someone," Dahlia blurted.

We all looked up from our plates.

"You did, who?" Charmaine said.

"His name is Paul. He works down the street from my job. He's a realtor. We went on one date."

"You went on a date?" I was surprised.

She elbowed me and said, "Yes, I went on a date. Finally!"

"Wow! He must be some guy because I can't even remember when you dated someone. Who was it? Oh, yeah, it was Robert." Jazz teased.

"Lord, is you sure?" Dahlia joked.

"I think she is right. There was maybe one guy after that. Lord, I know your sweet center got cobwebs. She hasn't been teased by a man in months," I said jokingly, but dead-ass serious.

"Ugh, I am eating, Miss Nini," Charmaine said.

"Nini?" Dahlia and Jazz said in unison.

"Oh lord, Char, why did you bring that up?"

"Who calls you that?" Jazz said.

"Who else but Michael I bet. I mean the man is mad cool but, Lord, I think he be trying to change you into something you are not," Dahlia blurted out.

I rolled my eyes. "Yeah, he does call me that. It's no different from baby, sugar, honey, and all that other stuff."

"I think it's cute,." Charmaine said.

"Well it looks like all y'all have passed me and I'm the one married," Jazz added.

All of our laughs and smiles disappeared when she said that. I didn't want to mention anything. But since the civil case had started she and Tim had seemed distant.

"What's going on?" Charmaine was the first to ask.

Jazz looked at each of us. "Besides the fact he doesn't come home anymore and he reeks of other women, nothing is wrong."

"Wait, Tim is cheating?" Dahlia said. "I had a strong feeling something like that was going on."

"Are you sure, Jazz?" Charmaine said.

"Oh, I'm sure. I don't have to see it to know. He is cheating and quite frankly, I pushed him to it."

"What you mean? I know you are not saying this is your fault," I said.

"Maybe it is. This lawsuit is kicking our asses. He never comes home and when he does, he sleeps on the couch now. I can't blame him. I pushed him to this point."

"I'm gonna kick his ass. That's bullshit, Jazz, and you know it," Dahlia said.

"Shh, Dahlia, please don't bring up that let's go-fight-the-bitch mentality. We are past that," Charmaine whispered.

"I got it handled, ladies. I promise," Jazz said.

"How? I didn't want to say anything but I saw a change in him. I also saw a change in you, Jazz. Y'all have Junior now. You two got to get past this," I said.

"Get passed what? The man cheated. There isn't any coming back from that," Dahlia yelled again. She was not helping the situation. "You knew it was only a matter of time before the old Tim came back. There was no way he was going to stay right forever."

"Dahlia, if you don't shut the hell up. Your negative ass is getting on my nerves. Everyone isn't Eric," I said, referring to Dahlia's ex who got her sister pregnant.

"Oh, are you going to take it there, Miss Nini? Look who you're fucking."

"Alright, Dahlia and Nitrah, both of y'all shut up. Don't start that mess again. This isn't even about y'all. Look at Jazz. We need to help her. Now y'all two shut the hell up." Charmaine slammed her hand on the table.

We all jumped at her reaction.

I looked over at Jazz and saw her tears. I felt bad for what she was growing through. But I couldn't say too much. I knew I was playing with fire knowing I was with Michael and creepin' with Troy. "What do you want us to do, Jazz? I am so sorry."

"Nothing. I'm fine. I decided to go to therapy."

"Therapy for what?" Dahlia said, and I was just as curious.

"You guys don't get it, do you? I'm not over it."

"Over what, Jazz? Talk to us," Charmaine said, rubbing her shoulder.

"I killed a man. He attacked me. Ever since then his family has been non-stop trying to ruin me, to tear me down. I got married because I wanted to be happy. I don't even know if it was right to marry Tim."

"You love him, Jazz, I am sure," I said.

"Yeah I do, but I'm not sure if I'm in love. Tim sees what I go through more than you all, and yet he still ran to the arms of someone else. Is that love? I don't think it is."

"I didn't know you felt like that," Dahlia said.

"Me either. I always thought you and Tim was this fairy tale. Something I believed in," I added.

"Well, we're not. Far from it. And I don't know if we can get back to being happy or even if I want to get back there. This therapy is suppose to help me heal and to open my eyes. I also decided to counter sue Terrence's family."

"A counter suit? On what grounds?" Charmaine said.

"Harassment and mental anguish. I think it's time for me to stand up and stop letting them run over me."

"Good for you, Jazz. I'm going to be with you every step to make sure you win that too," Charmaine said.

"Us too," Dahlia and I said in unison.

We all placed our hands in the middle of the table, holding hands all at once. These were the moments I enjoyed with my girls. These were the times when we were the closest.

Jazzaray Meadows

I signed in and took a seat closest to the door in case I decided to run. I was a little hesitant about going to therapy seeing as though I hadn't told Tim. I felt surprised that I told the girls about Tim's alleged affair, especially since I didn't have any proof. But a woman knows, and I didn't need any red-handed proof to know that my husband was back to his old ways.

The truth was I kind of felt relieved that he was home a lot less. I didn't care where he went, and he didn't care to offer an alibi.

The receptionist called my name.

I looked up, afraid to leave my seat. What was I going to say to the therapist? Would this even work? I didn't have any answers, but I knew I needed to speak to someone who didn't know me and couldn't judge me.

I got up and followed the lady down the hallway to the doctor's office. It was a big office on the eighth floor of a corporate building. It overlooked the main highway and the hills of Texas which were a few hundred miles out. The lady told me to have a seat and the doctor would be with me in a minute. I only had an hour session so I figured the doctor better hurry up. To my surprise the therapist was a man.

He walked in and said ,"Hello, I am Dr. Reed. How are you today?"

"I'm fine." I was reluctant to shake his hand.

"Surprised?"

"About what?"

"Well, a lot of my new clients always mistake me for a woman and by the tone of your voice, I want to make sure you are comfortable."

"I'm surprised but a little curious to see how this goes."

"Well, great. Shall we get started?" He took a seat in his lounge chair and offered me to lay down on his chaise lounge.

"Okey-dokey, I'm all ears," I said, as I lay my head against the chaise.

"Now, Mrs. Meadows, why don't you start off by telling me a little about yourself."

" I'm a student and I'm almost done with school. I am a mother of one son; a wife, newly wedded. I have three friends and two sisters; and, well, I guess that's about it."

"Great. So tell me why you are here."

"Well, I don't know how to start off really. I have been having some emotional problems and I just need to talk it out."

"Great, this is good, Jazzaray."

"Really? I barely said anything."

"But you talked. In my profession, it sometimes isn't so easy to get someone just to talk. So let's talk about school, what are you majoring in?"

"Journalism, believe it or not. I love to write. None of my friends really know that because I keep it hushed up. I don't know why, I just do. It seems they always have something going on."

"So they don't know your major or they haven't asked?"

"Both, and I changed it this semester. Mainly because I found myself writing more and I love it. I have been needing to write."

"Why is that?"

"Well … since, well, how can I say this? I was in an altercation."

"Explain that for me."

"Back in December, 2002, I was attacked by a former boyfriend of mine. He attempted to rape me, but as a result I—" I paused. I couldn't say the rest of it.

"What happened Jazzaray? Take a deep breath before you continue."

"I stabbed him in the chest and … he died."

"How did this affect you?"

"His family blamed me. They said I was the reason he was dead, which is sort of true, but I was being attacked." I felt myself becoming emotional. Tears started to pour out of my eyes.

"Here is some tissue. Take your time and relax."

"Boy, Dr. Reed, you sure are good. I mean ten minutes and I'm crying." I tried to make a joke of the situation.

"Jazzaray, it's okay to cry, let it out. When you're ready I will be here listening."

It took me almost ten minutes to continue and when I did, I made myself remember the day. I told him the story as I had seen it in my head a thousand times. "I killed him and I haven't been able to get over it. I married to make myself happy and look at the mess I'm in now."

"Have you told him these things?"

"Not in so many words. I mean in the past week we maybe have said three things to each other. I mean, doc, it is bad between us."

"You know you cannot make a happy future if you cannot let go of your past. Now you are suing Terrence's family. Do you believe that will help?"

"I don't know if it will but I hope they start taking me seriously now and leave me alone."

"Jazzaray, we are almost out of time. I want to give you an assignment. Usually I would wait awhile but we got a lot of things covered this session. I want you to go back to the place where the attack took place. I want you to go back there and face the past."

"You want me to go back there? I don't think I can do that."

"You can do it when you are ready, but this is a strong exercise that will help you. You must face this to get over it."

"When do you want me to go?"

"Not when I want you to go but when you are ready to go. That is when you need to jump in your car and go straight there without hesitation. I want you to write seven things you hate about it before you go. When you are there, I want you to place that piece of paper on the ground and leave it there. These seven things are the things I want you to leave behind."

"I will think of a time to do it, I promise."

"I have scheduled a session for next month. Jazzaray, have the willpower to do it before our next session. I have trust in you."

I stood up gripping my tissue paper. Thanks, Dr. Reed. I think I can do it. If I put my mind to it, I can get it done."

Troy Washington

So I was a little stupid with this hold Nitrah had over me. I didn't expect to see her so soon after she had finally cut me off. I thought about how I had left her over a year ago. How I had just disappeared and left her to fall into the arms of someone else. If only I was thinking and not being selfish, maybe I wouldn't be in this situation now where my former best friend is sleeping with my girl.

Nitrah must have thought I was a punk and that I was going to sit around and allow that to continue happening. She said she would fix it over a month ago and I haven't seen a change, just her dipping in both Michael and I. And I had decided that I was going to finally tell Teresa that she and I were done, until I saw that Nitrah was playing both sides of the fence.

I couldn't blame her, though. I was there once, struggling to finally be faithful to her. I couldn't give up Teresa or any of the other women I was with. Until Nitrah gave up Michael, I damn sure wasn't giving up Teresa. Period. So this was where we stood. Both of us knowing that we were still with other people and not saying a damn thing. This shit was starting to work my last nerve.

Nitrah had just called me up and said she was coming over to bring me something. I didn't know what it was or what it meant, but I knew that Teresa popped up all the time as if she lived here. My thing was I had to get Nitrah out of the house before Teresa came. Would that be easy? The hell if I knew. But I did know that Teresa and Nitrah in the same room was something I could not have on my hands again.

I prepared myself to act as if I were walking out the door as soon as Nitrah pulled up. That was exactly what I did when I heard her car. I walked down the ramp of my new townhouse and noticed Nitrah was in a different car.

"Hey, where are you going?"" she said.

"I was about to run to the corner store. Whose car are you in?"

"Oh this?" She smiled and said, "This is my car. Come on and take a ride with me."

I opened the door of her new Mercedes CLK. "This is your car, Nitrah?"

"Yep, I just got it today. Come on, let's take a ride to Hillsboro for some shopping."

"A new club, a new car, what else is new?" I said, buckling up my seat belt.

She pressed a button and the top let down as smooth as riding down an elevator.

"Oh shit, it's a droptop." Now I was excited. I was also wondering how on earth she was affording all of these things.

She pressed her foot hard on the gas after pulling out and yelled, "Hold on to your weave, boy."

The wind blew through our hair. Hers was recently cut short, which was something I also loved about her. It wasn't too short, but short enough to see the full length of her neck. She looked even more beautiful than the first time I saw her.

"How in the world did you swing this?" I said

"I got some funds saved up that's all. Why?"

"Just wondering. I thought all your money was going into your new club."

"It's more of a café."

"So what are we headed to Hillsboro to do?"

"Shopping, movies, dinner, whatever you want. Let's just hang out and have some fun."

"Just hang out, huh?"

"Yep."

"So, what have you been up to all week?"

"Working on some projects, the café, working with Jazz on something, and that's about it, and you?"

"I been looking for a new assistant coach all week, working with the team, and that's about all."

"Yeah I just need to get away. Lately, all I have been doing is working hard." I looked over at her and took in her demeanor. She seemed alright but her voice said something different.

We arrived in Hillsboro an hour later and parked in the largest shopping area this side of the Fort Worth. We shopped for a couple hours. We bought a few outfits, cologne for me and some shoes for her. We decided to drop our bags in her car and go out to eat. That's when I spotted Bennigans. "Let's go there." I pointed.

"Bennigans? Why?"

"Why not? It is where we first met. Well, not that one but you know what I mean."

She giggled and said, "Are you trying to recreate a moment?"

I took her hand and said, "Yeah I am. Come on." Her cell phone rang she looked at it and cut it off.

"Who was that?" I asked.

"Oh just my sister in Houston keeping me posted on a friend of mines there." I nodded I understood and we went inside of Bennigans.

***

The hostess sat us down at a table, and we sat across from each other. I admired the new ring she bought; it looked as if everything she wore was new.

"You look beautiful today," I said.

She brushed her hands across her hair. "Oh lord, why don't you stop it?" She was blushing.

"Okay, don't say I never said anything nice. I am just admiring you and seeing how everything is new on you."

"Well if you must be nosy, I got a huge check."

"For what?"

"A company signed me to a writing contract."

"A writing contract! That's good news. So that's why you are sporting the new car and the new diamonds." I joked.

She looked down and covered her hand. "Yeah, just something I am trying."

What's wrong? Let me see it."

"See what?"

"The ring. You know the one on your left hand."

She slowly lent her hand out to me and extended it over the table. I took her hand in mine and examined it. It was a large ring, nicely cut, several diamonds, and way out of Nitrah's budget. "So you bought this?"

"Not exactly. Come on, Troy, let's change the subject."

"Why? I'm just asking a simple question."

"Okay."

"Okay what?"

"Ask. What is it that you want to know?"

"Did you forget what you promised me a month ago?"

The server came to our table to take our orders but I waved him off.

"No, I didn't forget. I still stand by it."

"How, by sporting a ring you obviously didn't buy yourself?"

"It was just a gift."

"From who?"

"Troy, just drop it."

I hit the table with my hand. "From who!"

"Shh. Okay, it was from Michael. It was just a gift, nothing major. I mean come on. I know what I promised you. It's harder than I thought."

"You're playing with me, right? You're telling me that you wearing his engagement ring?"

"That's not what I said."

"You didn't say no either." I leaned back in my seat trying to hold back my emotion. I was trying to hide my anger. I was fed up. I didn't want to say anything else to her, because I was afraid of what I might say or do.

She leaned forward, crying. I looked up and saw her slip the ring off her finger. She placed it in the middle of the table.

"I'm sorry, Troy, I didn't want you to see the ring. I forgot to take it off. It is not an engagement ring."

"Did he ask you to marry him?"

She didn't say anything. I looked at her in her eyes and repeated my question.

"Yes and no. It is a difficult thing."

"Nitrah, do you not know how close I am to being done with you? I'm tired of you, seriously."

"Oh really? You're tired of me? How about I'm tired of you giving me ultimatums. As if I have to say what you tell me to say, do what you want me to do."

"What the hell are you talking about now?"

"You, Troy. I'm talking about you and your dumb ass. Here we are and yet again I let you into my bed, my heart, and my life."

"I thought that's what you wanted."

"I don't know anymore."

"How can you not know?"

"Stop pressuring me."

"Nitrah, you are the one who is sleeping with Michael and me. You are the one who is—"

"Me? Let's talk about you!" she yelled. "You left me, remember? You left and moved away. You didn't offer me a chance to explain myself. Didn't call or anything. Do you know why I can't get you out of my system?" She was screaming now.

The manager of the restaurant was walking toward our table.

"What, Nitrah? Is it because I left you and not the other way around?"

"You son of a bitch." She bolted, standing to her feet. "Well get this you ass. I can't get you out of my system because we shared a seed together."

"A seed?"

"Yeah, since you know everything and shit. I was carrying your seed. Your child."

"You were what?"

"I was pregnant by you."

"You were pregnant? Why didn't you tell me? Where is the baby

Dahlia Jones

I walked into my office, sat behind my desk and took off my shoes. It was one thing to have to look nice at work but I hated heels. I made a mental note to buy some flats.

Monica knocked on my door and said, "Hey, Dahlia, can I come in?"

"Sure, come on in. What's up?"

"I know we are almost off the clock and the work is almost done, so I wanted to know if you had a moment to spare?"

"Yeah, I actually do."

"It's a personal thing. Since I don't have any other friends yet, I thought I would ask you."

"Okay, shoot."

"I think I found the one."

"The one, what?"

"The man I want to be with."

"Already, girl? You move fast. You didn't tell me you were dating anyone. Who is he?"

"Well that's the thing. I can't tell anyone."

"Why not?"

"This is the advice I need because, well, he is married."

"Married? Girl, you should have asked me before you went there."

"I know, but I have a feeling he won't be with his wife for long."

"Why, did he say that?"

"No, not yet, but I am sure he will. We spend almost every night together, and the best part is we started off as friends."

"Monica, you need to be careful because these things never end well. This guy sounds like a dog for real."

"But he isn't. He is smart, kind, gentle, and he actually talks to me."

"Sounds like a man looking for something he is missing at home if you ask me. I don't want you to get overly excited because, well, men never leave their wives," I said.

"What do you think I should do to make sure he does?"

"Girl, I don't know. What I suggest you do is leave him alone until he decides what he wants."

"I figured you would say that but I wanted to make certain."

"So are you going to do that?"

"I'll see. I don't want to let him go."

"Monica, don't do anything stupid."

"I won't," she said, standing to her feet preparing to leave.

"By the way, Nitrah is throwing a party at her house, a barbeque and everything, next weekend. We are inviting a lot of people, so you coming? I hope to hook you up with a single guy."

"I'll think about it."

"Whatever. You are going and I don't want to hear anything else about it."

***

Paul called my phone. "Hey, Dahlia, are we still on for tonight?"

I smiled from ear to ear when I heard his voice. "You know it. I am so eager to go out and just relax."

"I have this spot I think you will like. A local jazz artist just opened it up, but it's in Dallas."

"That's cool. Me and the girls go to Dallas all the time. I'll be ready at seven." I hung up the phone to get ready to shower.

Paul was a new guy in my life. Someone I really didn't want to mention yet, but his name slipped out when I was at dinner with the girls. He was a very tall basketball type looking man. He was at least seven foot tall. Despite his large demeanor, he was as gentle as a cool breeze. I loved the time we spent together, and I planned to hang with him even more and take it slow. I also made a mental note to not introduce him to Joyclyn. I started my hot water when I heard my doorbell ring. I knew it could be anyone since it was a Friday night and everyone knew I was home. I looked through the peephole and it was Jazz.

I opened the door and said, "Jazz, what's up? What are you doing here?"

"I'm ready to go back."

"Go where?"

"I wrote the seven things down, and I'm ready to go. Can you drive me there?"

I knew what she meant when she said that. She had told us about the assignment her therapist had given her. I told her to call me when she was ready to go.

"Okay, give me five minutes. Here, take the keys and wait in the car." I ran through the house turning off my shower and redressing all at the same time. I dialed Paul and told him I would have to meet with him an hour later. I hurried and ran to my car hoping to not have changed Jazz's mind by taking too long. It was now in my hands to get her there and help her get over this.

***

We drove in silence. I played some Floetry through the system to relax us both. I felt as if I were the one who had gone through this ordeal. I knew Jazz hadn't driven on this side of town since Terrence died. I drove through the streets quickly, trying to not allow her to look around too much. I could feel her breathe in deep as I passed the daycare she used to work at, then the favorite place she used to love to eat at. I didn't want to ask her if she was okay because I knew she wasn't. I pulled up in front of South Glen Apartments. The same ones Terrence had died in.

"Are you ready? Do you want me to go with you?"

"No thanks, Dahlia. I got it from here. I got to do it by myself." She gripped the piece of paper in her hand and opened the door.

"Okay, well, I'm going to stand outside and wait by the car." I watched her get out and take each step. She was afraid and I knew it. I wanted to tell her that Terrence was gone and that he couldn't hurt her anymore. I also knew that what I said didn't matter, she had to believe it. I prayed this was a step in the right direction for her.

Jazzaray Meadows

I got out of Dahlia's car grateful that she was here. I also wished she didn't have to see me act like this. I knew it was just a building but the history it held for me was the killer. I walked up the steps leading to the second floor and gripped the rail. I was shaking so hard that I did not want to lose my balance. I couldn't bare Dahlia watching me so I yelled, "Come back and get me in twenty minutes."

"You want me to leave?"

"Yes, please. Just for twenty minutes on the dot."

"Twenty and I'm right back here, okay?" She hopped in her car and drove off.

I proceeded to continue up the steps with more courage now. Once I got to the top, I walked past two apartment doors and saw the numbers 401. That was Terrence's apartment. I deeply inhaled. *I can do this.*

I opened my piece of paper, looked at it one more time, and placed it under the doormat that was there. I turned around and hurried back toward the steps. I sat down on the top step to breathe because all of a sudden I was out of breath. I placed my head on my knees to take away from the atmosphere I was in. I was sitting in the same place the paramedics had found me in when they first arrived at the scene.

"Excuse me, Miss, are you alright?"

I looked up and saw a tall man. I instantly jumped.

He said, "I'm sorry I didn't mean to scare you. I just wanted to know if you were alright. You look a little shaken."

"I'm—"

"I didn't mean to bother you. I just thought you needed someone to say it was going to be okay."

I looked at him. He looked familiar, but then again Fort Worth was like that. Everyone was connected somehow.

"I didn't mean to yell. It's just that I didn't see you coming."

He stepped down a few steps and said, "Let me back up so I won't get assaulted by, Miss."

"Jazz. I'm Jazz and don't worry about it. If I was going to get you, I would of by now."

"Jazz. That's a melodic name. I'm Maxwell. I live in Apartment 402. Did you just move in? I haven't see you around."

"No, just visiting for the day. I'm leaving in a bit."

He laughed and said, "Wow, I scared you off that quick. Please allow me to apologize."

I giggled and said, "Maxwell, now that's a melodic name."

"Really? That's a first for me."

"It fits you. You know you got the dreads going on, the six-foot-seven stature and, well, you aren't that bad looking either."

"Miss Jazz, is you flirting with me?"

"Yeah, you're funny. I'm just stating the obvious."

"I guess I should say thank you."

"Yeah that would be nice." I joked.

"So you are only here for today. That kind of sucks since I'm enjoying our chat."

"I guess you caught me at a bad time."

"How about you reconsider that. I would like to take you out on a real first date."

"I don't even know you." I laughed.

"That's the whole point of going out. Come on. I promise the next time I will not turn you off."

"Wow, you are hilarious. But sorry. I'm going to have to decline the offer. My friend just pulled up and I think you already had a first date," I said, standing up.

He looked at me up and down and said, "You are truly one beautiful young lady."

I blushed and said, "Maxwell, you surely are a charmer."

"Man, this is our first date and I don't even get a number?"

"You are not letting up," I said, taking a few steps down toward him. I had to pass him to get to Dahlia's car.

"Okay, if I can't get a number, how about you meet me tomorrow?"

"Meet you, and where would that be?"

"I own a restaurant called Maxwell's in Arlington right off Cooper street."

"You're kidding me, that's you? You own Maxwell's and stay here?"

"Hey, I save money here," he jokingly said.

"I have been there a few times. I knew you looked familiar."

"Yeah, I think I used to know you too. So is it a date?"

"I'll think about it."

He extended his hand and said, "I sure hope you do. I'll be there all day. It was surely nice seeing you again, Jazz."

I shook his hand and said, "It was a pleasure seeing you again, Maxwell."

***

I hopped in Dahlia's car and she looked straight at me. "Ump, I thought this was an assignment and not a meet up. Who was Mr. Dreadlocks?"

"Oh, some guy who stays in the apartments. He just so happened to walk by and saw me sitting."

"Well, brotha is fine as hell. I love men with dreads like that, and he is tall. What is he, Jamaican?"

"No, I don't think so, but he told me he owns Maxwell's in Arlington."

"That four-star restaurant.? He has got to be lying if he stays here."

"He said it saves him money."

"You sure do know a lot about ole boy. Did you do the exercise?"

"Yeah I did, and I clearly forgot about it talking to him. He was really nice." I thought against telling her about his proposition to meet. But I was also excited that he had made me forget where I was.

"I must say this went better than I had planned. I was worried. I think I can make my date, too."

"You had a date? Girl, I am sorry," I said, as she pulled out of the apartments. I tried not to look back but I wanted to see Maxwell one more time, but I didn't want Dahlia to see me.

"Girl, please. You are way more important and you know that. Paul can wait."

"I think coming here helped me a lot. If it wasn't for Maxwell, I don't know how it would have ended. But look at me, I have a smile on my face." I laughed.

"Yeah you do, but I don't think it's from the exercise." Dahlia teased. "Watch out now Tim is crazy you know."

I covered my mouth and said, "Oh my goodness, I forgot all about Tim."

"What do you mean, like you forgot about him today or in general?"

"Sad to say, in general. I don't miss him at all and I never think about him. How did it get so bad?"

"You and Tim need to talk, finally. You need to tell him what's going on with you."

"I think I am passed that. He stepped out on our marriage and quite frankly, I don't want to go back. Take me to my mama's house. I can't dare go home after having a great night. Plus Junior is there. I have court Monday, so maybe I'll go home after that."

"Okay, girl, but remember y'all need to talk."

Dahlia drove me to my mother's house. Mama didn't bother to ask me why I was there. I went to my old room, Junior now used it when he stayed over. It was a Friday night and I had nowhere to go. I knew the girls were out with the ones they loved, and I was yet the one alone.

Tim was off work today. I knew because I called and he had been off for two days. It hurt in the pit of my stomach to know that he was a different man now. But most of all it hurt that I knew what he was doing and I didn't bother to let him know I knew. I couldn't remember the last time we laughed or the last time we made love. This was suppose to be my fairy tale ending. But that shit does not exist.

No one has a "happily ever after" because it was always some drama in it. I lay my head down and looked straight up at the ceiling. I thought about my life in the past two years. I thought about my son, my marriage, and then Maxwell. I don't know why he was even in my head. Maybe because I wanted that old schoolgirl-crush feeling again. Maybe it was because he was so easy to talk to and it seemed as if he was listening to me when I talked. No doubt he was different. Sexy too. But who was I to start anything with him? I just didn't care anymore. I wanted to be happy and today showed that I was ready. *I think I am going to take Maxwell up on that offer.* I could use some company anyhow.

***

The next day I hung around my mama's house. She made Junior and I some breakfast then I took him to the city park to feed the ducks. I tried to relax all day but I couldn't. I knew where I was going later that day. I wanted to go out and have fun.

Tim called my phone last night. I guess he realized I didn't come home. Maybe I never would. I can still hear his message in my head.

Hey Jazz, I am home and you and Junior is not here. Where are you? Give me a call as soon as you get this. Yeah right, give him a call. He left that message at four this morning. Bastard! The nerve of him to call at four, which clearly screams "I just got home". His ass hadn't even gone to work, and it made me sick to see that he wasn't even trying to hide the fact that he was cheating. Well, as the movie title says *Two Can Play that Game.*

Around three in the afternoon, I borrowed my mama's car and took off. I wanted to get me a new outfit. I hadn't been shopping in a long time, and I knew it was about the right time to do something for me. I had my nails and feet done then went to the salon and took my braids out. I did an out-of-my mind move when I cut all of my hair off into an old school Halle Berry look.

When the stylist was done, I turned and looked in the mirror and screamed out in excitement, "This is perfect." I told her I was satisfied with my transformation. I bought me a slick dress that fit all of the right areas. Bought a nice open-toe pair of sandals and a toe ring to match my necklace. I got into my mama's car and headed toward Highway 20, straight for Maxwell's.

When I got there the parking lot was full and the valet was letting people out of their cars. I drove up and handed one of them the keys. I walked up to the door and said, "Hi, is Maxwell in tonight?'

"I think he may be, who is asking?" one of the guards said.

"Can you tell him Jazz is looking for him? We were supposed to meet tonight."

"Hold on just one moment." He talked into his walkie-talkie.

I figured they were confirming my story.

The security guard laughed and said, "Yeah, he knows you. Go ahead and go on in. He says the hostess will have a table for you."

I felt good about the gesture. It seemed as if Maxwell had been waiting for me to appear. So I guess he wasn't lying, he did own this place. The scenery was just as nice as I remembered when I'd come here a few months back: dim lights, candle light, soft jazz playing, and the place was huge. Very elegant.

The host led me to a table behind a curtain. I guess this was VIP. She took my drink order and then was on her way. When she left, I heard her talking to a man behind the curtain and I realized it was Maxwell. I got the butterflies and immediately started to doubt the way I looked.

He pulled the curtain and stepped in and stopped dead in his tracks. "Jazz, is that you?"

"Hey Maxwell."

His eyes wouldn't go back in his head. He reached out for my hand and I stood up. He leaned in toward me and kissed me on the cheek. "Wow, I don't know what to say. I didn't expect Halle to show up and accept me on my offer."

I blushed. "Just trying something new for the first time."

"It does wonders on you I must say. Please do have a seat."

I sat down across from him and watched him examine me from head to toe.

"I can't believe how great you look tonight. What made you change?"

Really, was he asking me about why I had changed my hair and not criticizing it or was it a sexual remark? I was blown away. "I needed a change and to lift my spirits."

"I must say you look a lot happier than you did yesterday. I hope I had something to do with it."

"Honestly you did, and I want to thank you for being so kind."

"Little ole me?" He joked.

"Yes, little ole you." I giggled.

He turned around and said, "So order the highest thing on the menu. I want to make sure I keep that smile on your face."

"If you insist," I said, grabbing the menu.

I was surprised to see that he ordered and stayed with me the whole time. I figured he had to work. "So, Maxwell, you are dining with me and I am surprised you're single."

"I use to be married but that didn't work out. I have been divorced now for about two years. I try to live simple now so I won't attract the wrong women, you know?"

"Tell me about it. I'm trying to pick good men from here on out."

"So, I'm making you happier?"

"Yes you are. I think you are a natural. Why did you choose to ask me out on a date?"

"Why not?"

I blushed and said, "What I meant to say was why did you take interest in me?"

"I remember you from somewhere. I can't remember, but I do remember that I had a crush on you." He laughed.

"No, not you. Not Mr. Maxwell sitting across from me."

"Yeah I did, and yesterday I couldn't believe how unhappy you looked. I just wanted to cheer you up."

"I appreciate it. Really I do."

"So was the change in appearance a way to help you get over what it was that was bothering you?"

"No, not really. I just wanted to do something different for myself."

"That's the response I was looking for," he said, picking up his glass. "Look, I don't have to close tonight. Would you like to go somewhere else, somewhere people don't know me and I don't have to smile and shake hands all night?"

"Sure. What do you have in mind?" I said.

"I feel like dancing." He did a dorky move attempting to dance.

I covered my mouth and laughed. "Please tell me you can do better than that. You can't embarrass me now."

"Aw come on, you can teach me what you know."

"Well, I honestly rarely dance. But, hey, I haven't been to this place called the Jingles."

"Jingles off Smith and Towner? I have never been there."

"Then we should go. It's Saturday night. A great time to dance. This surely would be new for me."

"Ok well we can do it for the first time together. I imagine you drove. How about you follow me to my house to drop off your car and you ride with me?"

***

We did just that. This time around it didn't bother me to go back to the apartments that had changed my life. I honestly knew that what I was doing was getting close to someone else. I also knew that if I went all the way, there was no turning back. But most important, I knew I wanted to be happy. Right now, Maxwell was that for me. I hopped in the passenger seat and we drove to Jingles.

As we walked in, Maxwell grabbed my hand. I hurried and looked to see if my ring was off and indeed it was.

"I got to hold your hand if you don't mind," he said.

"Why is that?"

"Because that man over there keeps looking at you. If he didn't realize that you're with me, then he now knows. You see you are very tempting I might add," he whispered in my ear.

I instantly got wet, and my clit began to throb. *Oh my lord, he can do that to me with just a whisper.* "You must stop teasing me. You don't want to get into trouble now."

He threw his hands up in surrender and jokingly said, "Please forgive me. But it's hard trying to compose myself. That dress is screaming *Damn*!"

"Shh, you are crazy." I laughed.

"Okay I'll calm down. So what are those moves you were going to show me?"

I grabbed his hand and said, "Now it's time for you to follow me."

I walked him to the dance floor and stopped right in the middle. I hadn't been dancing in months, but I sure did remember how to move. That was one of my best qualities. I wanted to dance a little fast but the DJ immediately changed the music to a slower jam. Maxwell used this moment to move on in.

He whispered, "Do you mind if I place my hand right here?" He was insinuating at my waist.

My eyes told him yes he could. He wrapped his hands around my body and pulled me toward him. I wrapped my arms around his waist and rested my head on his chest since he was so tall. I listened to his heartbeat as his hands rubbed all over my back.

"I have never done this before," he whispered again.

I raised my head up and looked at him, "Done what?"

"Spent so little time with a person and be drawn to them immediately. I don't know what this is."

I lay my head back on his chest, afraid to continue looking him in his eyes, afraid that what I saw I would like. "I can't explain it either. But I love this."

"What?"

"I love the way I feel in your arms right now."

"Me too, Jazz. I could stay like this for a while."

I didn't say anything. I let a small trickle of tears fall from my eyes. I didn't want him to know I was crying. We stayed like that for twenty minutes, lost in our own thoughts, not wanting to say too much, not wanting to say anything to mess up the mood.

"This is a nice place." Maxwell was the first to break the silence. "But how about we head outside and talk? I would like to just get to know you."

It was well after two in the morning, but I said sure. He took my hand, again entwining my fingers with his. I loved the way he did that. The night breeze was cool as we walked the park area.

"I wanted to talk before, you know, we said our goodbyes. I didn't want you to think weird about tonight."

"Why would I? It has been wonderful thus far."

He stopped in his tracks. I looked at him as if I were trying to figure out what was wrong. I saw it in his eyes. He wanted to say one thing but chose other words.

"I want to kiss you," he said, turning to me.

"You want to kiss me?" I repeated. I suddenly was overcome with fear because this wasn't Tim.

"Yes, and I know we just met, but I would regret it if I didn't ask you tonight. I mean nothing has gone wrong tonight. This was one of the most perfect dates I have been on. I still don't want it to end."

My eyes filled with tearful emotions as I added, "You are right. I can't complain about anything. I am just so comfortable with you."

He let go of my hand and traced his fingers across my newly cut hair. "I like your new look. It fits who you want to be. I can tell."

I nervously took his hand from my hair feeling insecure. "You are too kind."

"Can I kiss you, Jazz?"

My clit started to throb again and I felt myself get wet for this man. I couldn't answer. I didn't know what to say. But my body said yes. I made sure he read my body and understood. He leaned in, not taking my lips, but looking me over in my face as if he was looking for something and searching my emotions. I leaned in closer to him and placed my lips on his. Our instant touch sent fireworks through my body. I was so emotional and so full of passion that I did not realize that our kissing escalated to tongue. He kissed me so passionately, so slowly, and so gently. He took my tongue into his mouth and gradually rubbed my lips with his. He was an awesome kisser. Then it dawned on me. I wasn't kissing Tim.

"Okay, hold on," I managed to say through breaths.

"I'm sorry. I went too far."

I guess he was referring to his hands rubbing all over my body. I guessed that we were close to doing more than just kissing.

"No you didn't. It's just I realized what we were doing. It's kind of fast and I like you, but I got to take in what I'm doing."

"You're right. I am sorry." He took a couple steps back and placed his hands in his coat pocket.

Why am I pushing him away when he wants to be with me? Tim obviously doesn't. "Come here, Max." I didn't realize I called him a nickname. "I mean, Maxwell."

He looked at me and said, "I like Max." He came back toward me.

"Let's head back home."

He took my hand and we headed for his car. I was so tired that I ended up falling asleep as soon as we pulled onto the highway.

***

"Jazz, we're here."

I heard Maxwell's voice. I looked up and saw Terrence's apartment building and screamed.

Maxwell grabbed me in a bear hug and said, "What's wrong? Look, it's just me, Maxwell. Nothing is wrong."

I looked up and saw him. My breathing became lighter.

"Jazz, are you okay?"

"I'm sorry, Max. I forgot where I was."

"Look, you're scaring me. Are you okay to drive home? It's almost four in the morning."

I didn't want to drive and risk going to sleep at the wheel but I knew I couldn't stay. "I have no choice."

"I have an extra room. You can sleep in there. I don't want anything to happen to you. I knew we should have taken your car to your house."

I saw the sincerity in his eyes. "I don't know about that, Maxwell. I met you only yesterday."

"Okay, you sleep here, lock all the doors and I'll go get a room. I'll return in the morning."

That wasn't a bad idea. "You would do that for me?"

"Sure, I trust you in my house."

I agreed and we got out of the car. I closed my eyes as I passed Terrence's old apartment. I didn't want to see the number 401. I held onto Maxwell's shirt as he led me inside his place. The apartment complex was plain on the outside and the exact opposite on the inside of his apartment. He had some of the most expensive things I had ever seen. "Wow, this is beautiful."

"Thanks. I'll go grab a shirt or something for you to sleep in."

On his way back to the living room, he handed me some of his clothes. Then, I realized I couldn't stay in this apartment alone.

"Maxwell, I don't think I can stay here alone. I think I will feel safe if you stayed."

"Are you sure? I don't mind leaving."

"It's not that, it's just that I got history here and I don't think I can stand being here by myself."

"Okay, I tell you what, I'll go get some blankets and we can camp out here on the floor. Is that cool?"

"Yes." I watched him rearrange things and make a soft, big pallet for us to lay down on. I don't know why, but I felt comfortable around him. If he was an asshole, he would have shown it by now. But I know my girls would be screaming at the top of their lungs if they would see me right now. I knelt down and lay my head down on the side designed for me.

Maxwell did the same. He leaned over and kissed me on my forehead and whispered goodnight. I whispered goodnight back. Together we fell asleep. As if I had known him for years, I felt like I was in the safest place in the world, even being next door to the place where I had killed Terrence.

Nitrah Hill

I turned over and the sun beamed right in my face. I raised my hand over my eyes to block the sun. Yesterday was a bad day. I came home Friday night and stayed in all Saturday. None of my girls were answering their phones for whatever reason. I needed some consoling, someone to tell me that it was going to be alright. I rose up out of my bed and sat on the side. I contemplated if I should get up or lay back down. Michael had been gone on business for five days now, which was why I wanted to spend time with Troyon. That didn't plan out as I had liked. Yesterday, as I lay in bed, it was a nonstop rewind of the fight I had with Troy. As I sat there the events played over yet again.

"Nitrah, come back here," Troy yelled out as I ran out of Bennigans.

"Troy, leave me alone right now. I don't want to be bothered with your shit again."

"You can't just say that and walk away. Stop!" He grabbed my arm and turned me around.

I was crying hysterically. "Yeah, so what else you want to know?" I took the ring in my hand and placed it back on my finger making sure he saw me.

"Don't play with me, Nitrah. Take that shit off your finger."

"Whatever, Troy. I knew I couldn't let this shit go. It was eating me inside."

"What happened? Please just tell me. I am here now. I got a right to know."

"You got a right? Boy, please. Stop with the BS. You don't have anything to do with whatever I did."

"What did you do? What happened to the baby? Tell me you didn't do what I think you did."

"What you mean, kill it?" I screamed. "Is that what you want to hear? Nah, how about I was going to have it. How about I went as far as not wanting anyone to know I was pregnant by your sorry ass that I didn't do anything about it. I let it grow inside of me."

"I'm sorry, Nitrah."

"Ugh, don't say that shit again. Are you sorry that I lost it? Are you sorry that I went into labor at five months and it died? Are you sorry that no one knew? I didn't tell anyone because of how they would look at me. I mean, come

on, getting pregnant by sorry-ass Troy, the one who left. I can hear them saying it now and laughing in my face."

Troy tried to grab me by the waist. He was crying. I didn't care what tears he cried, because I had to go through what I did alone.

"Babe, I'm so sorry I wasn't there. I'm so sorry. I am not going to do it again. Please, Nitrah, calm down. We can get through this."

"I already went through it. I tried to get over you and to get you out of my head. Why are you even back? What are you here to do, more damage? To cause me more pain? So what I fucking tricked you into dating me back then. We were all childish; but, shit, I am so over that I can't even bare to think about it. But hear this, I am not going to make you use that as a way to continue to try to run me and my decisions. Yeah, Michael proposed and you know what, I might as well be with him because I know he won't leave me."

"No. Does it look like it? Aren't I here now?"

I walked to my car and opened the driver's door. "Hop your ass in so I can drop you off."

He opened his door, afraid that I would leave him behind.

As he sat down, he placed his hand on my leg. "Nitrah, if you don't know by now, I am sorry. I want us to be together. Do you not know how hard it is to hear that we had a child and that I wasn't there? It's killing me right now."

"What was I suppose to do? Call your brother and say can you please give me Troy's number because I'm pregnant with his child? Do you not know how it felt to have you sleep with me and be gone the next morning, to only see you

a year later? You don't see what you have continued to do to me and for me to still love you is making me sick." I pushed his hand away.

He plopped back into his seat as I pulled out.

"I am seriously going to drop you off and force myself not to call you."

"I get it now. I can see it from your eyes." He slyly wiped his eyes. "I see why you act the way you do toward me. I finally get it."

"Oh you do now. It took that much?"

"I don't want you to leave me. I want you to leave Michael. I know you are angry with me. I can understand now why you do the things you do. But I get it now. You told me and I get it."

"It's not that easy to just say it. I have to want to do it."

He leaned over and grabbed my hand. "Nitrah, I am saying this now: I don't care how long it takes, but I want us to be together. If I have to tell Michael that I will."

I looked at him to see if he was serious. "Troy, don't say anything to him. It's my decision."

He sighed. "I'm going to stop talking but like I said, I get it. I'm going to live the rest of my life making this up to you. I promise."

***

It was eight in the morning. I figured I needed to go to church because I had been slacking. I got up, dusted off an old church dress, and drove to Greater New Light Missionary.

***

After church I decided to take a run in the park. I kept my commitment to exercise and I needed to make sure I was far away from my phone. Obviously Troy knew me too well. I guess a whole day of non contact made his butt drive over to my house and since I wasn't home, he tried the next best thing: the city park where I normally run.

"Stalking me now?" I said as I ran toward him.

"It's a nice day out so I figured you would be here." He handed me a bottle of water.

I took it and opened it up to take a drink. "Yeah I see. So what do you want?"

"Nothing. Just came to see you, that's all. I wanted to know if I could take you to dinner tonight. Something nice, my treat."

"No, I don't think so. I want to just hang at home."

"Okay that's cool too."

"Alone, Troy."

His face showed disappointment. "Well, you want to do something later in the week?"

"No, not really."

"Look, I have been struggling with what happened. I just want to know we are okay."

"Troy, I'm starting to heal. I am trying to move on as best as I can."

"Honestly, me too."

Now that shocked me a little.

"I thought a lot about what you said and I pretty much did all this," he said.

"What?"

"I remember when I first met you. I would have never told a woman I loved her. I couldn't even stay faithful to you then, because I wanted to stay a player. Then I leave you as if I didn't do anything wrong and now this. Like I said, I just wanted to make sure you're okay."

"Okay, now you're scaring me."

"Don't feel like that. I just get it now, you know. I get why you say the things you say. Why you didn't choose me over Michael. I just wanted to say I'm sorry." He turned around and opened his car door.

"I get the feeling you are leaving again," I yelled out. I had that feeling that he was about to disappear again.

"No, I told you I wouldn't do that again. But I also don't want to hurt you anymore." He climbed in his car. He suddenly stepped back out and closed his door again. He turned around and walked toward me.

"What's wrong?"

His pace didn't stop. He walked up to me and gently hugged me. He titled my head up toward his face and gave me a small perk on the lips. "I'll call you later."

I nodded my head in agreement. Something about him was different. Did I do this to him? Did I make him completely different and not seem like the normal Troy?

"Troy," I yelled out behind him. "I'll give it a try."

He turned back around with a small smirk. "Can't resist me, huh?" He joked.

"Let's just start over. But I still don't know what I want to do."

"I'll give you your time."

Tim Meadows

I drove over to Jazz's mother's house. It had been two days and Jazz hadn't come home or called me. She went as far as turning off her phone and now it was going straight to voicemail. I didn't know what was going on with her. Maybe it was because I stopped asking. I went as far as to forgetting that I was a married man. I had been sexing Monica down on a regular, so I hadn't noticed my wife. *How did I let it get this far?* I pulled up and saw they were here. I could see Jazz's sister, Lorraine, in the yard playing with Junior and her son. I parked and got out.

"Hey son," I yelled out, trying to get Junior's attention.

"Daddy!" he yelled and ran into my arms.

I got emotional, realizing that I hadn't been with my son in days.

"Hey Tim, we didn't know you were coming over today," Lorraine said.

"Hey Lorraine, I just came by to see my family, that's all. Is Jazz inside?"

"Yeah, she is in there helping Mama cook I think, or in the shower. Go ahead, I got Junior." She took him out of my arms and walked to the backyard.

I walked up to the front door and knocked.

"Who is it?" I heard Mama yell out.

"Hey, Mama, it's me, Tim."

"Tim, boy, come on in. You don't have to knock."

I opened her screen door and walked back toward the kitchen. "Hey Mama." I reached out to give her a kiss on the cheek.

"I was wondering when you were going to finally appear. Jazz has been here for days now. I am not the one to butt into grown folks business, but I am not dumb either."

"Yes, Ma'am. Where is Jazz by the way?"

"She is in the shower; sit down so I can talk to you."

I took a seat at her kitchen table and prepared myself for a lecture. "Okay, Mama, what's up?"

"Son, I am no idiot, and I went through this same mess with my husband. I have been praying for you and Jazz, but you two have to pray together. I don't know what's gotten into you two. You both got that boy out there that depends on y'all and here you two are living in a divided home. This girl is over here going through this lawsuit and her husband ain't here. Now I ain't ever been the one to chastise you, but you need to step up."

"Mama, it's just a lot of things going on that we need to work on."

"You sure are right. Get y'all butts back into church. Y'all need prayer. I'll be back, let me go find my blessing oil." She walked around the corner and down the hallway.

I heard the bathroom door open and I got nervous because I didn't know how Jazz would react to my being here.

"Mama, where is the lotion?" I heard Jazz yell out. "I am running behind and I got to hurry up and get out of here."

"It's in the living room," Mama yelled back.

I knew she had done that to send Jazz straight my way. I prepared myself to see her. I heard her footsteps coming toward me and as she turned the corner, I took a double look. "Jazz!"

"Tim, what are you doing here?" she yelled out in surprise.

I stood up, overcome with attraction to her. She looked ten times better and more beautiful than I could ever remember. "You cut your hair?"

She brushed the back of her head and dryly said, "Yeah, what are you doing here?"

"I came to see you. You wouldn't pick up the phone. What's going on?" I tried to talk to her seriously, but for the first time in weeks I had a hard-on for her and wanted to sex her right then and there. She looked so sexy in a dress I had never seen her in before.

"I'm about to head out. I'll try to come by later on today."

That hit me kind of hard. Why was she talking to me as if I wasn't her husband? As if we didn't live together and share a home? "Wait, I haven't seen you in days and I don't get a hi?" I extended my arms in hopes she would come and give me a hug.

She rolled her eyes and sarcastically said, "Hey Tim, how you been?"

"Jazz, can we talk outside please?" I knew that she knew something was up with me. I really didn't even try to hide that I was doing something secretive, but I didn't dare tell her I was cheating.

She turned around and I almost died when I saw her ass in that dress. *When in the hell did she get this fine?* We went outside and she sat down in the chair on the porch.

"So, Tim, what's up?"

"You changed. You look very sexy."

"Ugh, what is it, Tim? You really got to hurry up. I got to go."

"Go where? Why are you in such a rush to leave looking like that? You look like you're going out."

She looked down over her outfit and examined herself. "Well, I am. I'm just having a little fun."

What she said sounded dirty. Now I was getting upset. *Who was she going out with?* "I think we should talk about us. We let our relationship get way off course. I can't remember the last time we were happy."

"What are you talking about? Don't I look happy?" she replied. She honestly did look happy. Her face had this glow. Then it hit me, she was happy but it wasn't because of me.

"Yeah, you do look happy right now. But why aren't you at home with me?"

"I think I should be asking you that question."

Wait, does she know about Monica? Did I slip up and she found out? "I'm sorry I haven't been home. I just felt like you didn't want me there. You stopped talking to me. You wouldn't even let me touch you."

She looked down at the clock on her cell and said, "Look, I'll call you tonight."

"Call? What do you mean, call? Why aren't you at home? I want my family back at home right now."

"Tim, when you decide to come home yourself, maybe I'll consider it. But right now I have plans and I don't want them interrupted." She stood up and I stepped in front of her pathway.

"Where are you so eager to get to?"

For the first time she looked me in my eyes. We were almost nose to nose. I realized the happiness in her eyes. But when she looked at me, it disappeared. Despite being mad right now, my heart started to beat faster at just the sight of her. Having her near my lips and my body sent me over the edge. *Why didn't I notice this before?*

"Tim, did you forget about your double-dipping? You think a woman like me doesn't know." She touched my shoulder and told me to have a seat. "Listen to me, Tim. I am no fool, and I don't share my husband. You, on the other hand, decided that you didn't want to be a husband anymore. When I was hurting, you decided to leave me at my lowest point. Now I am standing here wondering why all of a sudden Tim wants me to be his wife? Why every time you have looked at me I can see your dick sticking out of your pants? Do you think I don't know you? Are you honestly going to be in my face and act as if I am your only one? Like I said, I got plans. And quite frankly, I don't think I'm coming home."

I listened attentively to every word she had spoken. She shocked me with each of them. I felt embarrassed as she read me like a book that she herself wrote. She knew me all too well. The fact she knew I was creepin' now justified where I knew she was going. She had found someone to make her happy. "Jazz, I'm—"

"Tim, if you say I am sorry, I promise you I am going to pop you right in your mouth. Better yet, I am going to punch you in your throat if you even try to look innocent. You did this, Tim. Why when

I was at my lowest point in life you leave me so easily? I don't want a man like that. I need my space." She folded her arms across her chest.

"Jazz, I still want us to be together. I can't stand my wife and my son not being home. You two are my life."

"Wrong! The bitch you fucking became your new life. You disgust me. I can't even see myself sleeping with you again after knowing you been with someone else. More than once!"

Jazz's mother came out onto the porch. "You two, I heard enough. I think you two need to calm down before this escalates."

"That's okay Mama, Tim was leaving. Better yet, take Junior with you. I think he forgot what his daddy looks like.'"

"I'll leave, but I am coming back. Mama, I'll take Junior."

Jazz jumped into her mother's car and drove off without saying goodbye.

In the room Junior used as his, I collected some of his things.

Mama walked in and said, "I am praying for you, Tim, because you are going to need it."

"Thanks, Mama."

"Now two wrongs don't make a right, but you need to know your wife didn't return to my house last night. You caused that girl to start living different. She thinks different and now is walking around here looking like a Halle Berry."

"What you mean she didn't come home last night?" *That's why her phone was off.*

"What I mean is I think you have a broken home and you need to turn to God for guidance. You single-handedly pushed that girl into the arms of someone else."

My heart dropped as Mama told me this. I knew what I was doing was wrong, but I didn't want my wife to be touched by another man. The thought of a man's hands on my wife's body made me furious. This wasn't supposed to happen this way. I plopped on Junior's bed and placed my head in my hands and cried out. I didn't know what else to do but cry. Mama came over and sat beside me and wrapped her arms around me. She went into one of her praying rituals, which in some form made me feel a tad better.

Jazzaray Meadows

I climbed in my mother's car and headed out before Mama or Tim could say anything else to me. I didn't want any drama after having a great couple of days, which I wanted to continue. Before the new week hit, Maxwell wanted to take me out on the town. I met him at his place and we hopped in his car. I didn't want him to pick me up because of where I was staying. I made a mental note to act like Jazzaray Harris and not Jazzaray Meadows. We stopped and parked in front of a nice retail store where I normally shop.

"Why did we stop here?" I said.

"I got an idea. You go in that store and I'll go in this one." He pulled out a wad of cash. "Buy whatever you like but make sure it's something real casual, something you can get dirty. I'll do the same thing too."

"Something I can get dirty?" I said, while taking the money out of his hand.

"Yeah, trust me on this."

I nodded my head. I was still confused, though. But I went in the store anyway. I bought some tight-fitted shorts, a halter top, several skirts, and a few midriff shirts. I got some matching sandals and a few more toe rings. I went into the dressing room to decide which one of the outfits I was going to wear. I decided on a bright orange halter and blue jean shorts. My phone beeped and I realized I had a text. Maxwell wrote that he was waiting in the car.

I walked outside after being satisfied with my outfit and spotted Maxwell. I hopped in as he said, "You really trying to tempt me, huh?"

I giggled. "What did I do?"

He pulled out. "I'm just admiring the way my girl looks that's all. You're sexy as hell."

I laughed out loud. "Clearly you are trying to sweeten the pot. Keep it coming."

He laughed too and said, "Okay, I will not feed the ego. But you are going to be surprised when you see where I'm taking you. I figured you could use a little excitement and have some fun screaming."

"Screaming, are you trying to get nasty with me?" I teased.

"Nope. But soon. Very soon." He licked his lips and proceeded to turn the radio up as an old Jon B. song played. I sat back and enjoyed the ride. Before I knew it we were on the road headed straight to Six Flags.

"You are taking me to Six Flags?"

"Yep, I haven't been in about five years. I thought we could both use the excitement."

"Oh lord, now I feel like a kid in the candy store. I haven't been here in ages. Maybe in high school."

"This is the reason why we needed to change into something else." He laughed. We parked his Lincoln Navigator and headed toward the ticket booths.

***

I honestly rode the majority of the rides, which was rare since I hated heights. But Maxwell begged me to go. Even though I was scared, I didn't regret doing it. We had so much fun I forgot about the ordeal that had taken place with Tim. It was honest to say that we were in fact over. I was trying to move on. Maxwell was a good way to move.

We stayed at Six Flags until it closed then headed out to get some takeout to eat back at his place. I was very tired from walking all day. So I knew this downtime with him would be much needed. When we got to his place, he placed the food on the stove and went to take a quick shower. I was going to do the same. My phone beeped, it was a text message. I sat down on the couch to read it. It was from Tim.

It read: *I was just thinking about you and wanted to let you know I still love you.*

I typed back: *I am a little busy right now. But I will call you tomorrow.*

I hoped he would leave me alone for the rest of the night. I was wrong because it beeped again just as Maxwell opened the bathroom door. I turned my phone off.

"Hey, Jazz, the shower is all ready for you."

I grabbed my bag of clothes and went to the bathroom to shower. I shocked myself even more when I realized how comfortable I was with him to bathe in his house. I stayed in the shower longer than expected, clouded with emotions I didn't know were in me.

***

Maxwell had reheated the pizza and wings we ordered and popped in a movie by the time I got out. "Dang, babe, I was starting to worry about you." He had his dreads down and a white T-shirt on. He looked very sexy and he wasn't even trying to look the part.

"I love showers, what can I say?" I unwrapped the towel from around my head. "I know you didn't eat up all the food."

He threw a pillow at me and said, "Naw, it's in the oven staying warm. See, I was trying to be nice and look at the thanks I get."

"Max, please." I giggled and threw the pillow back at him and went to retrieve my plate.

We ate and watched the movie *Sprung* and drank homemade margaritas.

Maxwell started laughing. "I think I'm the man in this movie."

Confused I said, "What you talking about?" I was laying out on his big couch while he lay below me on the floor.

"The man in this movie is similar to me."

"The photographer? How?"

"I'm sitting here watching this movie, but not really watching it. I'm realizing that I am a little sprung in just a couple days." He laughed slyly.

My attention was now focused on the back of his head. "What do you mean?"

He rose up and turned his body around to face me. He did so very slowly as if he was contemplating his next move. "I met you when? What, three days ago? And all I think about is you. We have spent like almost every hour together since then; and, yeah, I am looking at this movie and seeing myself in that guy." He pointed toward the character in the movie.

I knew what he meant. I had seen this movie when it came out almost ten years ago. The main couple fell in love in a matter of days and practically moved in together. "Are you trying to say that you are sprung?" I swallowed hard. Now I was looking straight into his eyes.

"I'm saying I'm falling for you, Jazz."

I wanted to scream out in excitement but as excited I was, I was also scared. Not only was he saying he felt the same as I, I knew I had a husband. Maybe Tim did cheat; and, yes, he had done me wrong. But the fact was I still held his last name. "Max, are you serious?"

He threw his hands up and said, "Don't go running away now. I am just speaking what's in my heart. I like you a lot; and, well, watching the movie made me realize that I want a lot of days like today and yesterday. I want days like that with you."

I swallowed hard. "You don't know how long I have waited to be happy. I just wanted to smile. I haven't smiled this much in months. I guess I can say I feel the same, you know. But at the same time I don't want to rush or jinx it."

He sat down next to me on the couch. I scooted over and made some room.

"Jazz, I know what you mean and just like you, I don't want to push it."

I allowed my leg to hang down over the couch, nervously shaking.

Maxwell noticed my nervousness. He placed his hands on my leg. "I am nervous too. But, hey, if I was a jerk, you would know, right? At least by now I hope so."

I placed my hands on his and said, "I think you are a good guy."

He scooted close to me, bringing his body inches away from mine.

"I'm going to kiss you now," he whispered inches away from my lips.

I breathed in deep as I prepared for his lips to touch mine again. He pressed them against me so slow, so gentle with such ease as if he wanted to savor the moment. He brought his hand up to my chin, bringing my lips closer to his. He began to use his tongue and lick every inch of my mouth, sucking and kissing my bottom lip. I moaned in between kisses as his body started to press up against mine.

He pulled back and said, "Do you mind if we take this to my bedroom?"

I didn't think about the question I just wanted more of what he was giving. He stood up and took my hand and led me down the hallway. I was surprised to see such a large king-sized bed.

He turned around and gave me a peck on my lips and said, "I am going to make tonight about you." He picked me up in his arms and swung me in the air and placed me down in the middle of his bed.

I could feel my clitoris stiffen with excitement as a warm sensation started to roar through my body. Maxwell stood at the end of the bed and pulled his shirt over his head revealing his very well-trimmed chest. His biceps pulsated and expanded. I could now see the depth of his physique. He was very well-built. He walked to the other side of the room and turned on jazz music. I giggled at the thought of him playing jazz for Jazz. I saw him go into his side draw and pull out some body oil.

"What are you going to do with that?" I asked.

"Shh, just relax. I got you." He jumped up on the bed and told me to pull my shirt off. I did, keeping my bra on in the process. He poured some oil in his hands and started to massage my feet then my legs and my thighs. I could tell he was going to go higher and higher. He reached my thighs and brushed his hands across the opening of my shorts. I shivered at his touch. My body was boiling. He took his hands and placed them on my shorts buttons. "May I?"

I nodded in agreement. He began to unbutton my shorts, sliding his hands underneath them to pull them down. I felt the pulsation in my clitoris as his hands passed over my ass. He threw the shorts onto the floor and poured some more oil in his hands and told me to turn over. I knew I had on a thong and that my ass would be exposed, but I shyly turned over acting as if maybe he wouldn't notice it. That thought left my mind as his hands started to squeeze and massage it. He ran his hands from the full area of my ass to the tip of my shoulders. I felt his manhood throbbing through his pants as he pressed against my lower back.

I jumped at the tingle when I realized he was licking every inch on my back down to the crack of my ass. My toes curled as the sensation of his warm tongue explored my body. He turned me back over and started to kiss my lips while massaging and pinching my nipples. I could tell my juices were escaping my vagina as my panties began to get wet. He removed my bra and began to suck and lick my nipples until they hardened so much that they began to hurt. I moaned and squirmed at everything he was doing to me.

My mind was going a mile a minute. I was making love to a man that was not Tim. I quickly erased that thought out of my head to fully enjoy the treat that Maxwell was giving. He rose up on his knees and removed my panties. He jumped down and hopped out of his pants and pulled out a condom from the drawer. When I saw that gold package, I was like *yes, he is well- endowed.* He hopped back on the bed.

We stared each other in the eyes. I couldn't help but take a peek at his penis. Making sure that what he was working with would make me scream at the top of my lungs. As he entered me, I could tell he was larger than my eyes perceived, or maybe I was tight because I hadn't had sex in a while. Once he fitted in, I felt my whole world go into a daze.

Maxwell pushed and moved. He made sure he introduced himself to all the wells of my love. He turned me on my back, my side, and finally had me on top. I rode him like he was a brand new ride. He cupped and held on to my breasts so that he wouldn't fall off as we connected with each other on another level. I screamed out as I reached my peek, letting him know that he indeed did tickle my pussy. The connection we made was so over the top that I didn't remember ever having sex with a man and it feeling like this.

Now I knew for a fact that I could not return to Tim and that I had to tell Maxwell about my situation.

***

The next morning I woke up to the sound of Maxwell showering. I wanted to call and check on Junior before he returned. I got up and wrapped a blanket around my body and ran to the living room. I turned my phone on to feel it buzz. I opened it up and remembered that Tim was texting me last night. I clicked opened my messages and it read: *I know you are having an affair.*

I dropped the phone in shock. I was scared about the outcome of my actions. What was I going to do now?

Nitrah Hill

Today I dressed in my corporate gear. Jazz decided to drive her car to the courthouse today, so I told Dahlia and Charmaine to ride with me. I knew after this hearing we would need to go out to eat and talk about whatever went down. When I picked up the ladies, we were all dressed up as if it was our court date. We needed to support Jazz, and I guess we felt we had to look the part too. We found a parking spot in one of the downtown parking garages and got out to walk. It was a four block walk; none of us were happy about walking in heels.

Inside the courthouse we walked through the metal detector, had our purses examined, and were finally allowed to go through. We started to look for Jazz immediately.

"Wait a minute, is that Jazz with short hair?" Dahlia pointed out.

"No, that girl looks like a young Halle. That's not her," Charmaine said, looking around.

Then the girl turned our way. I stopped dead in my tracks. "The hell it ain't, that is Jazz."

All of our mouths hit the floor. We were surprised at how beautiful and young Jazz looked again. We all walked up to her and I said, "How are you doing?" I knew I shouldn't have asked that stupid question, but of course I did.

"Well I'll be damned. We got a new hot chick in the click now y'all," Dahlia joked.

"Hey ladies, I am doing great." She reached out and gave us all a group hug.

"I am just shocked at how you look, girl. Is it me or do you have this glow?" Charmaine pointed out.

"No, I see it too," Dahlia said. "What has gotten into you, girl? I have got to change my look now. Nitrah and Jazz done went and cut their hair."

"Nothing, I just know today is going to be a good day that's all," Jazz added.

"I hear that. So is Terrence's family here?" I asked.

"Yeah, they are all inside."

"Where is Tim?" Charmaine asked, looking around.

Jazz shrugged her shoulders and said, "Don't know; but, hey, I am about to go inside. The lawyer wants me to be in before the rest of the crowd shows up."

"Okay, we are going with you."

When we all walked in, we saw Terrence's family's side was full of people. Then again, I made sure Jazz's side would be full too. I saw a familiar face in the crowd. "Dahlia, isn't that your coworker Monica?"

"Where? Oh yeah, I see her. I told her we were going to court today. I didn't know she was going to show up. I'll talk to her later."

We all walked toward the front row and noticed Tim, Robert, and Troy sitting there.

"Oh my goodness, I see Tim has brought the clan with him," Charmaine whispered.

I reluctantly took a seat next to Troy, not really wanting the ladies to know what was going on between us, but I promised him I would try. Dahlia sat on the opposite end of me and I imagined it was to avoid Robert. Jazz didn't bother to look our way.

"Nice to see you ladies made it in. Where is Jazz?" Troy said.

I pointed to her standing in the front near her lawyer.

"That's Jazz?" Troy raised an eyebrow.

"Naw, that couldn't be her," Robert said, jokingly.

"Yes it is," I said.

"Wow, Tim, I know you tearing it up at home," Robert joked.

Tim gave a sly smile, never taking his eyes off Jazz.

"Man, she has changed. She sure does look happy for this to be such a serious day," Troy said.

"We have faith that everything is going to be alright," I said.

"Damn, Troy, can you stop speaking on my wife?" Tim frowned.

"Shh, y'all this is a courtroom," Dahlia whispered. "Can't we all act civil?"

I looked over to Dahlia and saw Monica tapping her on the shoulder. "Hey Dahlia."

"Monica, hey." Dahlia stood up and gave her a hug.

I extended my hand and said, "Hey Monica, thanks for coming and showing support. That is real kind of you."

Dahlia looked toward Tim and said, "Hey, Tim, scoot down so Monica can sit by us."

Tim looked at Monica then at Dahlia and said, "Naw, there is Terrence's family's no room. I need space."

I shrugged my shoulders and looked back toward Monica and Dahlia. "Well, girl, just sit behind us then. You can join us after the hearing." I saw a weird disappointment in Monica's face as she searched for a seat in the row behind us.

"All rise!" The bailiff was now in the courtroom addressing the crowd.

We all stood up and waited for the judge to come in. It was an old black woman. I heard Dahlia whisper, "Girl, we got a sistah on the bench."

"Shh, that doesn't mean anything," I said.

We all sat back down and listened to the opening statements. Terrence's family had a good lawyer, and I was stunned at some of the things they said and the stunts they pulled. They made Jazz sound like a criminal. I could barely hear sometimes because Dahlia wouldn't shut up. She had a comment to say about everything. I was more than surprised by Jazz's lawyer. She was well worth all the money we put together to pay for this. I was positive we would win. I couldn't help but notice the longing in Tim's face. Something was going on with him, but I couldn't put my finger on it.

***

The judge set the next hearing for August 2nd. I was hoping that would be the deciding factor. We all sat outside the courtroom and waited for Jazz to come out.

"Tim, aren't you suppose to be in there with Jazz?" Charmaine said.

"I'll wait for her to come out."

"Hold up, is it me or is something going on with you two? Now I am not the one to butt in—"

Everyone laughed in disagreement.

"Okay, maybe I do butt in, but I know that you haven't been on the good end lately," Dahlia blurted out, pointing toward Tim.

Tim shot her a look as if he wanted to punch her in the mouth.

I interceded, "Dahlia, not here, not now. And shut up please."

Troy went over to Tim. I could see him whispering something to him.

"Man, I thought this would be a happy reunion." Robert joked.

"Happy? Robert look where we are. In a courthouse because these trifling-ass fools won't leave my girl alone," Dahlia blurted again.

"Dahlia, please calm down, and please shut up. I am not trying to be escorted out," Charmaine said.

Monica walked over to us and said, "So, ladies, the hearing, in my opinion, went great. I think you all are doing a great job supporting Jazzaray."

"Thanks. I think it's kind that you're here," Dahlia said. "Don't you agree, Tim?" she yelled that loud enough for him to hear.

"Dahlia, leave me alone. What the hell are you talking about now?" Tim said.

I watched Monica look over at Tim. Now I am not a psychic but this chick was really rubbing off on me wrong. I got a strange feeling from her, and the way she looked at Tim was weird. I elbowed Charmaine and whispered in her ear, "Do you see Monica?"

"What?" Charmaine was too obvious.

I had to whisper lower, "The way she's looking at Tim. That girl got something about her. I am telling you to watch that chick."

"Girl, please, that's Monica. We barely see her anyhow."

"I am just saying, Tim, you can be happy that we are all here to support. Look at me, I ain't said not one thing negative to them over there." She pointed toward Robert and Troy.

"Look, I'm going to go get my car. Tim, I'll meet you outside, alright?"

Robert knew when to leave because once Dahlia got started, she wouldn't stop until she got all she had to say out.

Troy walked over to me and kissed Charmaine and I on the cheek then told us he would talk to us later.

"Oh, you don't see us standing here?" Dahlia said to Troy, referring to her and Monica.

"Dahlia, don't even go there. You know damn well you don't want me near you."

"Shit, I am just saying. You acting all rude like us two aren't standing here."

Troy walked over toward her and said, "Look here." He placed both his hands on Dahlia's arms and kissed her on the cheek. He did the same to Monica.

Now Charmaine was elbowing me. "Look at your man doing something abnormal."

We giggled. Dahlia looked as if she had gotten hit by a car.

"Happy now?" Troy turned around and walked away. He looked up at me and Charmaine and winked.

I fell out laughing. *This man is really changing.*

"Wow, talk about the nice guy," Charmaine said after he was gone.

"I'm headed to the bathroom to wash my face," Dahlia said before walking off.

"Come on, don't be like that," I yelled after her, still laughing.

Jazz walked out and we all walked up to her. Tim was the first to stand up.

"So how did everything go?" Charmaine said.

"It went well. I'm excited about the outcome that's all. Why are you all still here?"

"Waiting on you to come out." Tim was staring her down.

I had the feeling they needed to be alone. "Look, you all, let's go out to eat and let Tim and Jazz be alone. I know you two needs to talk."

"Fine. I'll go and get Dahlia and we'll head out," Monica said, turning away.

I really didn't want her to come with us but I remembered Dahlia saying she didn't have any friends.

"Yeah, I'll call you all later and give you an update. Come on, Jazz," Tim said, pulling her by the hand.

I could see the tension all in Jazz's face. She cringed at Tim's touch. They walked off and I couldn't take my eyes off them two.

"What the hell is going on?" I asked Charmaine.

"I was just about to ask you the same thing. Now I sound like Dahlia. I don't want to get in their business, but they are our friends and what I saw in Jazz's eyes was not love."

"We have got to talk to her; it's like she changed over night."

"Yeah. When do you want to do it?" Charmaine said.

"I guess during our monthly meet up. I can't hold my tongue for long." I really wondered what the hell was going on.

"Yeah, so that means I can ask about you and Troy." She teased.

"Oh lord, let me walk away now."

"You can't run forever. I want all the scoop."

Tim Meadows

I walked Jazz to the coffee shop next door to the courthouse. She immediately let go of my hand when we got outside. I didn't argue with her, because I knew why she didn't want me touching her. When we got inside, we sat at a table across from each other. She turned her body away from mine, focusing on the people walking outside. I knew this talk wasn't going to be easy.

"How did we get this far?" I asked her. I wanted to break the silence. The attraction for her was there, the love I had for her was there, but I didn't know if she felt the same. "Jazz, can you just look at me?"

The smile she had planted on her face all day was now gone. When she looked at me, I felt she didn't like what she saw.

"Tim, will you cut straight to the point, please?"

"I am sorry."

"Sorry for what? You wanted this. You lived every day as if you wanted me gone. You didn't want to be home and you chose to step out on me. We have been married what, a year? I am just disappointed, Tim. We used to be like this." She held her hand up and crossed her fingers.

"Yes, I am sorry for everything." I lowered my head in shame.

"Sorry isn't going to cut it. I don't have to put up with your bullshit and quite frankly, I'm not. I think we both know what we got to do."

I looked up at her and said, "What is that? I know you are not trying to say you don't want to be together."

"It was over the day you got into bed with someone else. What disgusts me is you didn't even try to hide it. You disgust me completely."

"I'm sorry I put myself in that position. It's just I felt like I was missing something. You went away from me. You left me before I left you."

"I was hurting inside. These people were trying to kill me emotionally. You couldn't understand that? How would you feel?"

"I'm feeling it now. Are you doing this to get back at me?"

"Doing what?"

"I know you are sleeping with someone else. Mama said you didn't come home. You don't answer your phone. I mean you dress different, talk different, and you always seem happy. But when you look at me I don't see that. If I'm not making you happy, then who is?"

"Tim, I'm sorry but I can't go back to who I was. I can't go back to being be unhappy and left alone. You didn't care then, so why do you care now? Is it because I'm not paying attention to you now? Is this something you feel you got to win?"

"Jazz, I messed up, but I love you and I love Junior. I want us to be like we used to be."

She finally turned and looked at me. I looked over her brown complexion, her new haircut, and the glow that beamed off her skin. She was beautiful.

"I don't want to. Tim I'm sorry."

I felt myself get emotional. The tears I wouldn't let escape my eyes now started to burn. Was Jazz sitting across from me telling me she didn't want to be with me anymore?

"Jazz, what do you mean? Please, baby, come on. I fucked up but I won't mess up again."

She now had tears coming out of her eyes. She wiped them away before saying, "Sorry, Tim, but I don't see you the same. I mean

I try, but how can I love someone who left me like that? You knew I was sick. You knew I had panic attacks. You knew of the lawsuit. You knew of the turmoil I went through after Terrence died. But yet you still were the one to hurt me the most. Of all the people in the world, why you, Tim?"

"Please don't do this, Jazz. I changed for you. I used to do a lot of bad shit and then you came along and changed me. I became a better man for you. I messed up. I am sorry, but please don't leave me."

"I just can't. Maybe I could take you messing up once; but, Tim, you left home every day to go off and do whatever with you know who. How disgusting can you be? It doesn't get any worse than that. To repeatedly fuck someone else and then sit across from me and say you're sorry, I deserve better and you know it."

"What can I do? I mean I will do anything. We can go to counseling."

"See, it shows how much you been there. I have been to counseling. When my husband was fucking off on someone else and I wanted to die because I felt all alone, I took it upon myself to talk to someone. You see I am sitting here today because that helped me. You didn't. You weren't even there."

"You went to counseling?" My heart almost shattered. How did I let myself get caught up into Monica so bad that I left my wife to fend for herself? I sunk lower and lower in embarrassment because the more Jazz talked the more I realized that I did more damage than I expected.

I threw my face into my hands, realizing that I was losing this battle. And if I didn't say something, Jazz would walk away from me. I started to sob like I have never done before. Hearing that my wife wanted to be happy without me made my heart pierce. It felt like someone was cutting me deep and trying to kill my soul. I heard her get up out her chair. I looked up. I was afraid she was walking off, but she placed a chair beside me. She wrapped her hands around my neck. I jumped thinking she was trying to choke me.

"Calm down, Tim. Don't make a scene in here. Look, we both are adults. We both know that we can't go back."

I wiped my eyes before I turned to face her. "Jazz, all I am asking is to take me with you to your counselor. Just one time."

She leaned back and exhaled. "Look, if it will help you understand why I need to move on, then yes. I have a date in three weeks. We can go together then."

***

I parked in front of Monica's place. I didn't expect her to show up at court where all my friends and family would be. She had taken it too far. I walked up to her apartment and banged on her door. "Monica, I know you're in here. Open the door."

She swung it open, clearly showing that she was upset. "You finally show up."

I walked in and screamed, "What the hell were you doing today? You are crazy to come around my wife like that?"

"What are you talking about, Tim? I am your number one—not Jazzaray, and you need to see that."

"This is crazy. You have gone too far with this shit. Stop asking me to leave my wife. We've been fucking, what, a month? This is ridiculous. I'm not leaving my wife for no one."

"You just don't see it yet." She went over and sat down on the couch. "But you will in time, I know it. We have been together almost every day for like two months."

"Look, Monica, I know I have said somethings to you, but I wasn't thinking right, okay? I think what we are doing is done. I got to focus on my family now. Jazz knows."

"She knows about me?"

"No, she knows there is someone else. And now she. My words trailed off.

"She what?" Monica stood. She was pissed.

"She is having. She's sleeping with someone else."

"Good. So now it's settled, you can move in here."

"What? Did you not hear what I said to you? I'm done."

She came toward me, and I prepared myself to restrain her if she got physical. "You and I belong together. We are perfect for each other. I have no one else. You are it for me. Now, don't you see that?"

I leaned up against her front door thinking about the next thing I should say. I didn't want to hurt Monica because she had done so many things for me. She actually listened to me when I needed to talk. Then again, I should have been talking to Jazz.

Monica whispered, "Can't you see, Tim, we are meant to be together." She came closer to me. She pressed her body up against mine.

I could feel the temperature in the room rise as she started to rub her hands over my chest. "Monica, this has got to stop. We got to think about what we are doing."

She didn't say anything else. She started to kiss my neck and my chest. My body surrendered to her touch. She knelt down and unzipped my pants, taking all of me in her mouth. I stood there unable to resist temptation. I watched her taste me and guide me into the depths of her mouth. Leaving her alone was going to be harder than I thought. How can I explain to Jazz that the woman I'm sleeping with is Dahlia's friend?

Nitrah Hill

August 2004

It was early in the morning. I had a lot of work to do on my new building. Everyone who was anyone was coming to help me work on it today. I asked everyone to come on a Saturday mainly because no one had to work. I had already resigned as a full-time teacher. I didn't have to worry about money too much since I signed a lucrative writing deal with Sista Lit. Magazine. I was now a contributing writer and columnist. I felt my life was going in the direction that I needed it to go, although I did still have problems in the romance department.

I pulled up in front of my café and parked. I got out and noticed a large suburban truck. Instead of being nosey and wondering who it was, I walked to the door to go inside until I heard.

"Nitrah!"

I turned around and Michael was running up to me. I dropped my bags overcome with excitement and ran to him. I jumped in his arms, smothering him with kisses from ear to ear. It had been a month since I had seen him. His job had taken him to Spain to speak to potential athletes for American teams.

"When did you get back?"

"This morning, I just got in." He turned around toward the truck and waved the driver off. He picked me up again and swung me around in the air. "Baby, it is so good to see you."

I squeezed his neck tight. I was overwhelmed with excitement and emotions. I had missed him so much. But also while he was gone Troy and I were like the couple we used to be before the scam.

"Oh my goodness, I have missed you to death." He twirled me around while looking at me from head to toe. He took my left hand and kissed the ring he had put on my finger. I guess he wanted to see if it was still there.

"How did you know I would be at the Café?"

"I called Charmaine and asked her. She said everyone was going to be here in about an hour. So instead of going home to sleep, I'm here, and it's a perfect time to see everyone too."

"Come on, I want to show you what I've done with the place so far."

We walked into the café and he admired some of the things that were done to the place. He was paying for everything out of his pocket. I loved him for that but I also felt guilty.

"Wow, babe, you have done a lot of things. We are almost done."

"Yep, we just got to work upstairs and in the bathroom area." I heard the front door open and a female voice say hello.

We both walked back to the front and I saw Dahlia and Monica.

Her again. What is she trying to do, become a part of our click? I didn't too much care for Monica, because I knew something was up with her. But I put on my fake smile and greeted the ladies. "Hey ladies, you guys are on time."

"Hey man, when did you get back?" Dahlia said, walking up to Michael for a hug.

He reached out and hugged her and said, "This morning. I heard everyone was coming in."

Monica walked over to him and said, "Hey, Troy, right? Yeah, I think we met a month ago or so."

Dahlia elbowed her and said, "Naw, girl, this is Michael."

I am going to kick her ass.

Dahlia immediately looked at me with apologetic eyes.

"Yeah, I'm Michael. Why would you get me mixed up with Troy?"

Monica stuttered and said, "Oh, I think I heard the name or something. Don't really remember."

I turned away so Michael wouldn't see my face or my guilt. I felt he was about to say something when the door opened again.

"Hey baby sis. I'm in the house. Where is the VIP section?" I turned around and saw my brother Jailen.

"Hey bro, you didn't bring any of your females with you? We can use the help?" I tried for dear life to change the subject in hopes that Michael moved on from Monica's statement.

"Yeah, she in the car putting on makeup," Jailen said.

"Makeup. Lord, you brought a pretty girl. She can't be pretty up in here because she is about to work." Dalia joked.

I laughed at Dahlia and noticed Michael walk out the door. He stood out there talking on his cell phone. I knew he was upset.

"Hey, Jailen, go get your girl, will you?" I said, shooting him out the door. I turned to Dahlia and Monica. "Thanks for having a big mouth. Don't say anything else, okay?"

"Sorry, I didn't know. I promise. I thought that was him," Monica said.

Dahlia said, "Sorry, Nitrah, I tried to help. But, hey, it's over. Michael will understand the mix-up. Everyone knows about Troy."

They walked off and proceeded to find something to do.

Dahlia ran back to me and said, "Oh shoot. I think Charmaine said Troy was coming."

"Oh my goodness. I forgot. I didn't think Michael was going to be back. I got to go call him." I ran to the front of the store and what I saw made my heart sink. "Dahlia?" I screamed, never taking my eyes off of my front door.

Out of breath from running, she said, "What, girl? You are scaring me."

I couldn't talk. I didn't know what words to say. Dahlia turned her head and said, "What is the news station doing here?"

"That's what I am trying to figure out." I saw Jailen and Michael speaking to the reporters. They both knew each other very well because they both worked for the Mavericks basketball team.

"Wow, looks like your brother and Michael have set up an interview for the café'. Is we going to be on TV? Let me go put on my face." Dahlia ran off and grabbed her purse.

I started to do the same thing. I looked up and saw the news crew come in.

Michael was talking to them. "This will be the main floor, and the stage will be set up over there. The upstairs will be set up like a lounge and have a second bar. To your right you will see the entrance way to the outside eatery we will set up. Oh, and everyone this is Nitrah Hill, an up-and-coming writer, a spoken word artist, and, yes, fellas, she is taken." He walked over to me and wrapped his hands around my waist.

The news reporter said, "Well, Miss Hill, you have taken the city of Fort Worth by storm. How does it feel to have the only poetry café in the city?"

I tried to sound professional. "You know it's something I am still trying to wrap my head around. This has been in the making for a while now. I know the people in the city will love it because we don't have places like this. I mean being so close to Dallas no one has took the initiative to open a poetic café, especially if it's geared toward African Americans. But here they will get what they need for the soul."

"So when should we expect a grand opening?" The reporter said.

"I don't want to jinx it but in sixty days, perhaps."

"So, Miss Hill, tell us what the name of the newest spot in the city is."

I didn't know the name; I was still stuck on what to call it. Then it came to me. I had the perfect vision for it. "Lyrical Lounge."

The reporter turned to the camera and said, "There you have it. The Lyrical Lounge is creating a hot buzz throughout Fort Worth. Make sure you come out to 1500 Main St. and experience a new kind of atmosphere. This is Tanya Wright for Fox news, back to you David." Tanya turned around and said, "Thanks, Michael, for the exclusive. Miss Hill, it was a pleasure. I will be back for sure."

"Thanks so much. I appreciate it." I was overcome with excitement. After they left I gave Michael and Jailen a bear hug. "You guys are too much."

"Don't give me credit, Michael did all that." Jailen gave Michael a handshake and went off to work alongside his girlfriend.

"A surprise, huh?" I said to Michael.

"Well, I knew I would be here today." He smiled. He was so handsome and for some reason I didn't remember him looking this sexy.

"Hey y'all sorry we are late." Charmaine and Jazzaray walked in the door.

"You two missed it, the news was here," Dahlia said before I could.

I felt it was a perfect opportunity to take Michael off to my back office and mess around a little. I pulled his arm. "Come on and follow me."

He giggled and said, "Babe, come on, there's a lot of folks here."

"So what. I haven't had you in a month, now come on."

As soon as he closed my office door, it was heated. Michael pulled open my blouse and greedily grabbed my breasts with his hands. We kissed each other rough and fast and with so much passion. I knew I shouldn't have been sleeping with him too, but he was doing so much for me and I loved him. I felt it was only right. I slid my jeans down over my legs and turned my ass toward Michael, pushing my tail into him.

He dropped his pants and moved my panties to the side and entered with me with so much force that I jerked. I bit my bottom lip so I wouldn't scream out with passion. I gripped my desk because I did not want to fall off and Michael used my waist to keep his balance. I threw my ass back and expanded my legs so he could go in deeper. I felt him reach the deep end. I couldn't hold it and I screamed out in ecstasy. Michael brought his hand to my mouth and covered it. I moaned out and asked him to go in deeper. He did. As soon as it started, we were exhaling from our orgasms. I began to breathe heavily trying to catch my breath.

"Damn, babe, you were ready," Michael said in between pants.

"I was ready." I turned around and kissed his lips.

We washed ourselves in my adjourning bathroom.

"Do you hear that?" Michael said.

"No, what?"

He opened my bathroom door and then I heard voices.

"That, it sounds like people arguing."

"It sure does."

We pulled up our clothes and walked back to the front. I almost tripped over my own two feet when I saw Troy standing there. Dalia was trying to get him to leave.

"Troy, what the hell is you doing here?"

Troy looked directly at Michael. I could tell he wanted to hit him. Then he looked at me. I pleaded with my eyes for him to not step out of line.

"I didn't know you were back," Troy said.

Troy read my body language. I saw the disappointment in his eyes. I knew what was going on in his head.

"Why would you want to know I was back?" Michael turned around and looked at me.

I looked away in shame. I hate that I was the reason why Troy and Michael weren't best friends anymore. But I didn't start a relationship with Michael until two years after they had stopped talking. I told myself over and over to not feel guilty.

"Look, I just came to help out," Troy said.

"We got it from here." Charmaine looked over at me. She mouthed the word sorry.

"Yeah I can see I'm not needed. I guess I will catch you all later."

"Were you here to see Nini, is that what is going on?" Michael turned around and looked at me again.

I instead looked at Troy, and Michael looked from him to me. He was trying to read us.

"Who is Nini?" Troy was clearly confused.

"Nitrah. Are you here to see Nitrah?"

"I was here to see everyone. We are all still cool. If you don't know by now, maybe you should ask someone." Troy was getting an attitude.

Michael looked around the room; I could see his temples pulsating. He was getting more upset by the minute.

"Look, everyone calm down. It's obvious Michal and Troy can't be in the same room, so we all agree to make sure this doesn't happen again," Charmaine said.

"Cool, I will see everyone later." Troy took one last look at Michael. He said the words as if he were leaving but he didn't move.

"Boy, you better stop looking at me like that," Michael yelled.

"Alright, guys, just turn away from each other. Seriously no fighting." Jazz was now trying to play the peacemaker.

Michael turned and walked upstairs. The room was so silent we could hear each other breathe. My eyes followed Michael. I could see Jailen shaking his head in disagreement as if I needed him judging me. I looked back toward Troy and mouthed sorry.

He said, "It's cool, we all break promises." Then, just like that, he walked out of the building.

Not much work was done after that. The girls and I left. I told Dahlia to meet us at the Rhapsody, minus Monica. I just didn't like her.

***

"So, wasn't that awkward?" Charmaine was the first to speak.

We had made it into Rhapsody and were sitting on the outside patio drinking red wine.

"Yes it was, and I'm not too surprised. I knew it was coming," I admitted.

"I am sorry for Troy a little, though, to be honest. The brother just can't move on. That's not the Troy Fort Worth remembers. Shoot there is plenty of women who still talk about the former dog of the funk," Charmaine said.

"I think I may be living what you're going through, Nitrah," Jazz whispered.

Charmaine and I looked at her as if she had lost her mind.

"What the hell do you mean?" I said.

"Tim and I. Well, we're not so close anymore. Honestly, I think I'm done with the marriage."

"Wait, Jazz, did you talk to Tim about his alleged affair?" Charmaine said, placing her hand on Jazz's hand.

"It's not an alleged affair. He is having one. He has been having one. I guess Troy changed but Tim didn't."

"Wow, I can't believe Tim would do that. After all this time, why now?"

"I did push him away a little, especially since the lawsuit. But I never once thought about stepping out on my marriage until—"

"Wait is you saying you are cheating too?" Charmaine yelled.

Jazz didn't say anything.

"I guess we are in the same boat," I said.

"What the hell has happened to the value of marriage? Bobby and I don't do this shit," Charmaine yelled this time.

"Lord, Char, I know you are not cussing. Calm down. I mean, come on, Jazz and Tim will work it out."

"That's just the thing, I am done. I fell for someone else," Jazz said.

I threw my hands up in the air. "Who is he? What are you thinking? You are married and I am not. There is a difference."

"That doesn't mean anything. A heart is a heart and a vow is a vow. I don't want Tim anymore."

"This is wrong, you and Tim have to talk," Charmaine said.

"I set up a date for both of us to see my counselor. We go Monday. But I'm going to show Tim I'm done. He already knows about what I have chosen to do. Yet he didn't come home the same night I told him. I expected him to so we could talk. But he didn't even come home. Shows you how serious he is."

"I just can't believe this. So much is changing. Michael and Troy know I love them both. What am I suppose to do?"

"You know, ladies, you two need to spend time alone in my opinion. This is ridiculous."

"Shut up, Char. Ugh, I don't want to hear that right now. My husband cheats and I find happiness in someone else and you say negative shit like that. Everybody doesn't have a damn Bobby," Jazz said.

Charmaine turned to her as if she wanted to slap her. "Don't yell at me. I am not the one who is bed hopping."

"That's it." Jazz jumped up out of her seat.

Dahlia came walking up the stairs and Jazz bumped her in the arm.

"Ugh, excuse you, Jazz", she yelled behind her. She came and sat at the table. "So, ladies, what did I miss?"

I looked at her and folded my arms. "Drama as usual, you didn't miss anything new."

Jazzaray Meadows

I met Tim at the therapist's office since neither one of us was staying at the house. I planned to tell him that I was done and that I couldn't play being his wife anymore than he could play being my husband. Child together or not, I refused to be unhappy. I drove up in my Ford Focus and parked. At the same time, Tim drove up as well. I stood by my car and waited for him so we could walk together.

He walked over to me and reached out for a hug. I reluctantly gave him a small embrace and told him to follow me. I knew this day was not going to be a good one, but I knew what I needed to say. Maxwell had become a great part of my everyday life, and I didn't want to jinx that either. Inside we sat down on the same couch. I scooted over so Tim wouldn't get the wrong impression.

Dr. Reed walked in and greeted us. "Well, Mrs. Meadows, when you called and said your husband would be joining us, I was very excited. This is fast progress."

"Yes, Dr. Reed, I did everything you asked me to do. I did the exercise. I went back."

"You went back where?" Tim said. Clearly he was lost.

"Well, let's first briefly tell your husband why you are here."

I was glad that Dr. Reed suggested that because I had planned to lay it out on Tim hard.

"First I want to say I felt alone. I was depressed. My husband was off cheating. And, well, I wanted and needed someone to talk to."

Tim shifted in his seat showing he was uncomfortable.

"Okay, that's a blunt way to say it. I imagine, Mr. Meadows, you are here to listen but please feel free to chime in."

"Anyway, doctor, I went back to the place where Terrence died."

"You went there? Why didn't you tell me?" Tim said.

"Shhh, let me talk. I wrote down those seven things and to be honest one of them was my marriage. I wanted to leave the pain of that behind." Tim looked directly at me.

"Jazz, I am here because I want to work it out."

"That day changed my life. It has been a month of bliss I tell you."

Dr. Reed took notes and shook his head declaring that he was listening.

I continued on with my story: "I had enough courage to confront Tim about his creeping and I chose to not put up with it. You see, doctor, I have moved on. I want Tim to see and know this."

Dr. Reed looked up at me over his glasses and Tim stared straight into my mouth.

"Doctor, I am trying to tell my wife that I am sorry. That I'm here now."

"Really, Tim? Well, why the day after my court date you didn't return home?"

His eyes widened.

"Yeah, that's right. I actually went home that day. Our talk, after we had left the courthouse, had got me to thinking. I went home to talk to you some more. To my surprise you didn't even come home. Still fucking her, huh?"

"Now, Mrs. Meadows, let's keep this calm and civil."

"You went home that day?" He was stuck. He just looked at me with pleading eyes.

"Don't look at me like that, Tim. You just say what you want me to hear, but you are still young and immature. I don't have time for you to sleep with whomever and expect me to open my legs to you. For what, why would I risk my life and my health?"

"I am sorry, Jazz—"

"Shut up with that same ole line. You didn't mean it enough to not cheat again." I turned to Dr. Reed. "Doctor, help him understand that I am done. I'm happy now."

Tim got up and said, "Doctor, she is trying to leave me for someone else. I know it."

Dr. Reed said, "Is that true, Mrs. Meadows?"

I proudly said, "No I am not leaving him for someone else. I am simply with someone else. Point blank."

"I don't think infidelity will cure the way you feel. I think you both need some counseling together to work these issues out," Dr. Reed said.

"No, doc, I disagree. Ask Tim why he chose to cheat. Why he left me when I was mentally unstable? He wasn't worried about his son or my well-being."

Tim got down on his knees and looked me straight in the eyes. He asked me again to just work it out.

I bluntly said, "I can't. I don't see you the same. But I do want to be friends."

He yelled out in anger, telling me I was wrong and that I should at least try.

"Okay, I'll try, Tim, on one condition. I meet your mistress face to face."

He jumped up from his seat. "What?"

"I want to meet her. I want to see her face to face and talk woman to woman. If you can allow me that, then I will consider coming home."

"Why would that help? I don't think it will."

"And I don't want to wait a couple days. I want to go right now so you don't have time to prepare a lie. Let's get in the car together and go."

Tim plopped down on the seat and dropped his head. "I can't do that."

"Why not? It's very simple. You won't see her ever again so it doesn't matter, right?"

Dr. Reed said, "I don't know about that, Jazzaray. I think you two should talk it out more before you try to meet the other person face to face. I want you to try—"

I cut him off and said, "This is the only way I will come home. Why can't I meet her, Tim?"

"Because, it's just, well I don't want her—" He stopped talking.

I stared him down. "What's the big deal! I don't know her and she doesn't know me. It's not like I will see her again anyhow."

Tim grew quiet.

I bent down, my face only inches from his, and screamed, "I know her? Oh, you have done it now. Get your ass up and take me to her. I promise you are not leaving my sight until I see the bitch." All sorts of thoughts started running through my head of who it could be. What if it was one of my best friends? Names and faces started to run through my head. I went as far as to yelling out Joyclyn's name because she was always quick to sleep with someone else's man.

Dr. Reed tried to intercede. He went as far as to ask for security for Tim. I pulled Tim's arm and dragged him out of the doctor's office. I was going to meet this woman face to face and I was going to meet her now.

***

I hopped in Tim's passenger seat. I did not look in his direction; I did not say a word. This was going to happen whether he liked it or not.

"Jazz, I can't take you to go see her. I know what is going to happen once you do. I can't have you two fighting."

"Tim, understand this, if the woman didn't know me then I wouldn't have anything against her. But the fact that she knows me takes it to a whole other level. This is way beyond you, sweetheart. This is about respecting another woman."

"I can't take you. I refuse to allow this to go down."

"Who is she, Tim? Don't tell me it's one of my girls. I will go head over heels to find the bitch. I promise you all hell will break loose. Either tell me now or get ready for the ride." I sat back and folded my arms."

"I'll tell you," he whispered.

"What was that?"

"I will tell you but you got to stay calm. After this, you will come home, right?"

I gave him that *don't play with me* look.

He slouched back in his seat. "Monica."

"Monica who?" I played names and faces over and over in my head. "I don't know any Monica."

He looked at me with those pitiful eyes again and said, "Dahlia's friend."

I thought again and lightning struck, her face appeared in my head. I jumped and looked at him.

I screamed out, "Her?" I didn't realize I had punched him directly in his nose until I saw him grab it in defense. I turned around and push opened his door, disregarding the parked car next to us.

Tim got out and yelled after me, "Jazz, calm down please."

I didn't run fast enough because before I knew it he had a hold of my arm. "She was at the courthouse that day. She showed up at Nitrah's café. What the hell were you thinking?" I punched his arm repeatedly trying to get free.

"I don't know what I was thinking. I am sorry."

I screamed out, "I am so done with you. Lord, you have no idea how much I want to ring your neck. How could you do this, Tim? How could you choose her over your family?"

"If I could change what I did I would," Tim said.

I watched Tim fall to his knees and cry out. As much as I hated him and wanted to turn my back on him, I couldn't bare to watch him react like that. I had never seen him be so emotional, to cry so hard and so hysterical. I bent down and placed my hands over his and rubbed him in hopes to show him a little comfort. *Why the hell am I comforting him?* He looked up at me with his eyes red as they come and hugged me. I allowed him to hug me and to cry on my shoulder. I couldn't be too angry at him. I guess I played a part in us falling apart. Not a big part, but I didn't try to make it better either.

"Tim, look at me." I raised his head off of my shoulder. "I want you to calm down and I want you to listen to me."

He wiped his face and tried his best to act as masculine as possible now.

"I want you to hear what I have to say." I stood back up and brushed the dirt off my legs from the street. "We fell apart. We strayed away from our marriage and in the end, we made some of the biggest mistakes we could have ever made. But I am not in love anymore. I have moved on. Not because of what you did but because of where I am in my life. Personally, I think we need some time apart, and I think you are not ready to be a husband to me anymore. To be honest, we know what we got to do. We just have to except it."

He stood up now having the courage to face me. He placed his hands in his pocket. "I love you, Jazz, but if this is what you want, there is nothing I can do."

"Tim, we can make it, I promise you. I can be one of your best friends, but I don't think I can be your lover or your wife."

"So what now?"

"We move on." I extended my hand to hold his. "We move on and we raise our son." I leaned in and gave him a hug. I turned and walked toward my car. I yelled back toward him, "I will talk to you later, okay?"

He nodded his head and turned away. As much as I hated him I knew we had a son together, and I had to love him because he was the father of my child.

I pulled out my cell phone and called Dahlia. I called Nitrah and Charmaine as well as my sister Lorraine and told them all to meet me at Nitrah's. I had something to say and I didn't want to repeat it.

***

Everyone was there on time. They were on time because they were eager to hear what I had to say. I took some of Nitrah's juice out of her refrigerator and drank some before I spoke.

"Come on, Jazz, now spill it already," Nitrah said.

The ladies all agreed.

I exhaled and sat the juice container on the counter. "I am divorcing Tim."

They just sat there with the same look on their faces.

"Did y'all hear me? I'm getting a divorce."

"Yeah, I heard. But tell us something we didn't know," Dahlia said.

"I agree. Mama and I knew this was coming," Lorraine added.

Charmaine leaned back with her arms folded.

"Char, you don't have anything to judge right now," I said.

"Nope just listening," she said dryly.

Nitrah said, "So I guess you talked to Tim and you two went to the psychiatrist today."

"Yes we did, and I discovered who the mistress was, too." I looked dead at Dahlia.

Charmaine stood up with her arms in the air. "Oh lord, is it you Dahlia?"

"Hell no, why you looking at me, Jazz?" Dahlia yelled out in anger.

"Oh no, was it Joyclyn? Is that why you looking at Dahlia?" Nitrah said.

"No, it's not her thank goodness. But she is one of Dahlia's homegirls."

Dahlia's mouth dropped. "Oh my God, I didn't know. Which one, who is it?"

"Monica!" I screamed.

"What!" everyone yelled out.

"You are fucking with me, right?" Dahlia was furious.

"Hell no, he been sleeping with her a couple months now." I justified my statement.

Dahlia covered her mouth and said, "She mentioned something about being in love with a married man. I can't believe this."

"In love? The bitch is about to become familiar with my foot in her ass." Nitrah started pacing. "I knew it was something up with her."

"This is some mess. I cannot believe Tim." Charmaine plopped down on the couch.

"Well believe it. Tim and I are done. I have moved on."

"Are you going to tell them about Maxwell now?" Lorraine said.

"I wasn't until you opened your big-ass mouth and said something." I went and sat at Nitrah's table so they could all see me at once.

"Maxwell who?" Nitrah and Charmaine said in unison.

I had already told Lorraine about my relationship with Maxwell. I guess after a month of seeing him and declaring I was leaving Tim there was no need to hide it. "Maxwell is the man I'm seeing."

"You're serious about this, Jazz." Charmaine said.

I raised my hand to her so she would shut up. I didn't want to hear any negative preaching out of her mouth. "I'm dating Maxwell and he and I are serious. It's only been a month or so. But we really care about each other."

"Lord, have mercy. You and Nitrah need to decide what you want to do," Dahlia said, pointing her finger at Nitrah and me.

"Oh I know what I am doing. I'm going to be with Maxwell. You ladies can meet him you know."

"He is gorgeous," Lorraine said.

The ladies broke out in laughter.

"Lord, Jazz, if you can make a decision, surely I can too," Nitrah said.

"Pick Michael," Dahlia yelled out.

"No, pick Troy," Lorraine said. "What?" Lorraine looked at everyone and shrugged her shoulders. "I know all the details just like half the city." She joked again.

"I agree, pick Troy," I said.

"Lord, no, please pick Michael. Troy is so old news," Charmaine added.

"It's a tie. No help here at all." Nitrah laughed.

"I don't care about who Nitrah picks right now. How the hell am I going to face Monica without beating her ass and losing my job?"

The room got quiet as Dahlia took us back to serious mode.

"Let's get her when she least expects it. Let's get her where it hurts. Hell, let's get Tim too."

We all laughed and talked about our plan to hurt the woman who had hurt me.

***

"Babe, come on. I'm ready to go. We can't be late. This is going to be the night you meet my girls." I was pacing back and forth in Maxwell's living room.

He had tried on so many outfits I would of thought he was one of the girls. He was nervous about meeting the ladies I called my best friends. They were all in fact my sisters. Maxwell finally walked out of his room and was trying to put his tie together. It had been two weeks since I had broken off things with Tim. I had taken my ring off for good and practically lived with Maxwell during the week.

I grabbed my purse and opened his front door. "Finally. Let's go, slowpoke." I giggled as he raced behind me trying to grab his wallet and keys. I turned my head away and performed the same ritual every time I passed Terrence's old apartment. I grabbed the rail to walk down when Maxwell yelled from behind, "I saw that. I thought you just did it that one time. But this time I saw it."

I turned around and said, "You saw what?"

He caught up with me on the stairs. "I saw you look away from that apartment. Why do you do that?" He pointed toward Terrence's old apartment.

I looked away again. I placed my hand on his and told him I promised to tell him when the time was right. He accepted my answer and led me to his car. We hopped in and headed toward Dallas to meet everyone at Rhapsody.

It was a windy day for mid-August. Days like this made me miss my longer hair. I wore dress pants with a black satin blouse and black heels. Maxwell had his dreads pulled back, which was the norm for him. He wore a button-down shirt, tie, and slacks. When we got to the club, we let valet park the car.

Maxwell took my hand in his and whispered, "I'm nervous."

I giggled and said, "Don't be, everyone is cool. But then again, there's Dahlia. She is outspoken so if she likes you, everyone else will."

He nodded his head in agreement as we walked in. I looked toward the front desk and noticed they had a new poster of Nitrah up. This was her farewell performance before the grand opening of her club.

"Nitrah is performing tonight," I said to Maxwell, pulling his arm.

He looked over at the desk and said, "Wow, didn't expect her to be that beautiful. Is that the woman you mentioned whatshisname, Troy, is seeing?

"Yes, but I told you she is in a lover's quarrel so it might not be Troy tonight."

"Okay then. Well, let's find the crowd."

We walked inside the club area and it was very crowded. They had posters of Nitrah all over. I saw a news crew and a reporter from the new magazine Nitrah was going to write for. "Wow, I am so excited. I feel like I know a celebrity."

"Yeah this is pretty nice in here. Kind of gives my place a run for its money."

"Oh come on, babe, I see Charmaine." I pulled his arm and felt him stiffen up. I realized he was nervous again.

"Jazz, is that you?" Charmaine came over and gave me a hug.

I knew she wanted to be the first to see Maxwell.

"And you must be the special someone Jazz keeps talking about." She extended her hand and I was relieved at how nice she was being. Finally she wasn't grilling anybody.

"Yes I am him," Maxwell said.

I whispered in his ear as Charmaine yelled for the gang to come over, "Loosen up."

"Wow, he is fine, girl," Dahlia said as she extended her hand.

Maxwell laughed and said, "You must be Dahlia."

She raised an eyebrow and said to me, "What you tell this man?"

I raised my hands in defense and jokingly said, "Nothing, you are just an easy person to point out." I looked over her shoulder. "Is that Paul?"

"Yeah that's him." She yelled out again, "Paul, come over here and meet Jazz and Maxwell."

"Dahlia, lord, you are loud." I laughed. I pushed Maxwell toward the table and said, "Everyone, this is Maxwell, a special friend of mine."

"Hey Maxwell," everyone said in unison and they proceeded to shake hands.

Bobby was there along with a few of his friends, so I knew that this meeting would lead back to Tim.

"Where is Nitrah?" I said.

Michael walked up behind me and said, "She is meeting a lot of influential people. Tonight is her night."

He looked very handsome. He had the top button of his shirt open and you could see where his biceps almost pulsated through his shirt.

Michael proceeded, "The evening is about to start, so I'll speak with you all later. I have to walk with my baby and shake a few hands."

We all took a seat as a well-known jazz artist took the stage. Maxwell was talkative and fit right into the group. I was on cloud nine until I turned around and saw Troy and Robert walk in.

"Do you all see what I see?" Dahlia said.

"If you are talking about Troy and Robert, I see them as clear as day," I said.

"Robert and Troy Washington?" Paul said.

I guess he knew the history of them.

"They are coming over this way," Charmaine said.

"What, are you all surprised to see us?" Troy said as he made it to our table. "My girl is speaking tonight." He looked over and saw Maxwell. He introduced himself and took a seat at the end of the table. Now was it just me or was Robert staring Dahlia down?

Dahlia Jones

I was sitting down at the table next to my man Paul, so why all of a sudden did I feel a fresh pair of eyes on me? Probably because Robert was the one who owned those pair of eyes.

Paul didn't miss one beat. He interceded in this stare down that Robert and I had going on. "Hey, I don't think we met. I am Paul, Dahlia's friend."

"Friend, huh?" Robert said.

"Okay. So, guys, what's new?" Jazz said. She obviously didn't want any drama at the table.

"Nothing, just came to see our girls. I mean we came to see Nitrah perform."

I could tell Robert said that on purpose. I eyed Troy and signaled for him to control his brother. I looked over at Charmaine who had her head in her hands, clearly an indication of a headache.

"Yeah, well it's nice to be with my girl tonight and support her friend," Paul said never taking his eyes off Robert.

Bobby looked around and said, "Am I missing something?"

Charmaine said, "No, baby, just be quiet."

I looked away from the table. I was upset because I didn't know what was up with Robert all of a sudden. Then I saw Michael spot Troy. I looked to Troy then back to Michael then signaled to Jazz who did the same thing.

"I'll be right back," I said and jumped up from the table. I walked over to Michael and said, "Please be cool tonight; he is only sitting down with us. This is Nitrah's night."

"Why is he always here? Is there something going on with them, Dahlia?"

"No, of course not."

"He is just friends with all of us that's all. Like Nitrah was with Denim, remember," I said referring to Nitrah's former lover and best friend.

"I'll be cool," he said, putting his hands in his pocket.

I looked back and noticed Troy raise his head acknowledging Michael's presence. I turned and saw Michael do the same thing. Maybe that was an understanding between them. I looked behind

Michael and saw Nitrah walking toward us. The air left my lungs when I saw how beautiful she looked. I elbowed Michael and said, "Your girl is here."

I walked toward her and gave her a hug. "Congratulations, Miss Hill, you look fly tonight, Miss Thang."

"Thanks, girl. I had to. There are too many cameras here not to look sexy."

We laughed and hugged one last time. I turned and watched her and Michael embrace and in the back of them I saw Troy looked disappointed as he watched them pose for photos. Next to him I watched Robert get out of his seat. It looked like he was walking toward me. To make sure he wasn't, I walked toward the back some more. I peeped around the corner and out of nowhere he ran into me. "You scared me," I said, recuperating from screaming out.

"Sorry about that."

"What are you doing? Were you walking toward me? I moved on purpose to get out of your way."

He moved into my space. I eased backwards trying to gain some distance between us. We ended up inches from the exit door and no one was in sight.

"Robert, what are you doing? Why are you acting weird?" I put my hands on his chest, preventing him from moving forward.

He touched one of the loose curls in my hair and twirled it in his finger. "You look nice tonight." His lips were inches away from mine.

I felt my pussy jump as his warm breath brushed across my cheeks. I stuttered, "What are you doing, Robert?"

He stepped back and spoke in a serious tone, "Why are you with that guy? He doesn't seem right for you."

"I am going to ask you again: what the hell are you doing?" I was getting around to what he was hinting about. I was getting angrier by the minute.

"Seeing you with him brought me to reality."

"Stop right there. Who do you think you are?" I slapped his hand away from my face. "You mean to tell me you see me with another man and now what? What you got to say now?"

He leaned back even more. "I know I'm wrong but I couldn't resist getting you alone tonight. You just look so happy."

"Right, I am. So why are you here in my face speaking this bullshit?"

He pressed a finger against my lips. He leaned in toward me again inches away from my lips and said, "I just wanted to be alone with you, just to do this." He moved his finger from my lips and kissed me.

My pussy jumped again at his touch. Only he could give me this feeling. I pushed him away. "Robert, stop. Don't do this again.

It's been, what, a year and some months?" I angrily hit him in his arm.

He grabbed both my hands and pushed me up against the wall. He kissed me again with so much passion and so much force. He loosened his grip on my hands and brought them to my face guiding my lips toward him. I stood there and let him become familiar with my mouth and my body. He pulled away, clearly out of breath, and looked in my eyes. I stared back but was too afraid to say anything that could mess up this moment. I was also confused as to why he wanted me so badly now more than ever. He looked over and I followed his gaze to the back door of the club.

He looked back toward me and said, "Will you follow me?"

I was too weak to talk from the passion I had just experienced. I shook my head yes. We ran through the dark holding hands as if we were escaping captivity together. We made it to the lake a few blocks away from the club before we stopped running. I was so out of breath that I collapsed on the park bench. Robert sat next to me talking a mile a minute about how sorry he was. How he couldn't stand to see me with Paul and so on and so on.

"So what are you really trying to say, Robert?"

"Isn't it clear? I want you back. I mean it this time. I am over what happened a longtime ago."

"Okay, I got to get back to the club. I was crazy to follow you out here. They are going to know we are together." I stood up preparing to walk back.

"Dahlia, come on. We always seem to see each other and as much as I try to act like I'm over you. I hate to see you without me. I don't want to feel like that anymore. Forget what everybody says. Forget how my brother feels about us."

"Robert, this is ridiculous. You must just be caught up in the moment."

"Oh yeah, so why did you let me kiss you then?"

"Maybe I wanted to be kissed," I said, shrugging my shoulders.

"I know you want to get back together. I don't see why we shouldn't."

"Maybe because you said this before and we have been down this road. I don't know what's up with you and Troy. You two don't seem to know what you want until it's almost gone."

"I'm not worried about Paul. I know you don't really want to be with him."

"Lord, have mercy," I screamed and took off toward the club.

Robert tried to keep up the pace but even in my heels, I was not letting up.

When we reached the back door to the club, I said, "Don't come back to the table, okay? Please I don't want Paul to know."

"Only if you promise me one thing."

I rolled my eyes at him and said, "What?"

"I take you home tonight. If you don't let me then I tell everything." He jokingly threw up his hands to display telling the whole world.

Trying to hold back a smile, I said, "If you will keep your mouth shut, yeah, I can use you as my taxi tonight."

He pulled my arm and swung my body back into his. "I plan to do more than that." He kissed my lips again, and I swear that I almost lost my balance. He let me go and opened the door.

I blushed all the way back to my seat eager for the night to be over.

"Where you been at?" Jazz said as soon as I walked in their view.

"Walking around and mingling with people. It was a little tense here."

Paul eyed me. He was upset and not buying my story.

"Well, you're just in time. Nitrah is coming up. They just did a tribute to her."

I looked from Charmaine to Troy, who was blushing at me. I gave him the evil eye. Apparently, he knew why I was away from the table. He and Robert both had their own plans tonight.

Nitrah Hill

I was happy to see everyone I knew and loved. Jailen was here with his groupies hanging all over him. My sisters Tierra and Raven were here in the VIP section on the top floor and of course, my girls were here. I looked over and saw each of them seated next to their special someone. My eyes stayed glued on one of the sexiest men I had ever seen, Maxwell. I only looked for a split second and turned away. Lord knows that's all I needed was to be looking too hard at another man.

Michael was looking extra tasty tonight. He was shaved and wearing his beard mighty fine, showing his biceps through his shirt, and licking his sexy-ass lips. None of his good-looks prevented me from seeing Troy, though. If the night I first saw him in Bennigans was the night I said he looked his best, I was lying. He looked absolutely fine tonight. I got jealous when I saw several women approach him, but he charmingly turned them away. I felt guilty at how honest and faithful he was being to me. It made the night more intense as the two men I loved were standing in the same room yet again.

The tribute Rhapsody gave to me took those matters off my mind. They played old clips of me from when I first started open mic. I laughed at how much of an amateur I was compared to who I am today. Michael held on to my waste the whole night, declaring I was with him. The dress I wore was already tight-fitted but not as tight as his grip. It worked my nerve a little not being able to breathe. So I was glad when the tribute was over and I was free to walk up on the stage. The entire club roared with applause as I made my way to the stage. I shook hands and kissed cheeks thanking them for coming out. I was overwhelmed with how many people had come to support me and had come to support poetry in general.

The club owner came out on stage with me and held up my hand as if I were in the ring and I had just won by a knockout.

I took the microphone out of his hand and said, "Thank you all for coming, you have no idea what this means." I heard Dahlia's voice over the crowd yell something and I laughed and said, "Yes that's my best friend Dahlia being loud as always."

The crowd laughed out.

"Please, every one, have a seat. I am so thankful for every one who came out and supported me and Rhapsody. I mean I have so many memories here that you wouldn't believe. I witnessed some heartaches as well as some triumphs here." My memory went back to the night Troy found out about the scam. I breathed in deep to try to ax that memory out of my head. "I first want to thank all my good friends and my family up in VIP enjoying the free bubbly."

The crowd laughed out again. Before I could say anything else, I noticed Michael walk over to Troy and my heart started to race.

Stuttering, I said, "This has been an amazing night having everyone in here." I couldn't take my eyes off Michael and Troy because their conversation was getting heated. I saw Michael raise the front of his hand to Troy, displaying the matching engagement ring he wore.

I started to sweat so hard that I felt my armpits get moist. I heard the club owner yell from the side of the stage, "Nitrah, are you alright?"

I looked down at my engagement ring. I looked back up at Troy who was now standing by himself and watching me. The pain in his eyes made my heart cringe.

The club owner said again, "Nitrah, are you okay?"

"Oh sorry, everyone, I was caught up in my thoughts. I was just thinking about some of the people who inspired my poetry."

The club was quiet except for the music playing. I looked around and saw Michael standing across the room. I knew then I was going to change the poem I chose to perform. I looked back toward Troy and saw him walking toward the exit door.

I yelled out, "He is considered one of my best friends, someone I love with all my heart and he is here tonight. I hope he chooses to stay and listen because I wrote this with him in mind." I saw Troy stop in his footsteps. My heart skipped a beat.

He turned around and looked at me. I saw people in the crowd looking around trying to figure out who I was looking at.

"Do you all want to hear what I want to say? I know it's a night to reflect on what I did at the club, but I wouldn't be me if I didn't leave tonight without giving you an original piece, a tribute to someone who will always have my heart."

The crowd's attention was back on me as they cheered me on. I looked toward Michael who was clearly upset. I turned away not wanting to watch him become angry. At this moment I realized that I always catered to his feelings and not Troy's.

"This poem is dedicated to him and he knows exactly who he is. I call this, Complicated."

Baby

I wouldn't blame you

If you hated me

The things I've done

Decisions I've made

I can only imagine

How bad the pain stings

I know that you hate to be alone

Trust me

Despite the situation that I've created

At night

The lust and love speaks

Clutches me

I often have flashbacks

Visioning the sentimental moments

Of which you were touchin' me

All up in me

But I try to fight it

Only because my current situation

Plays a factor

I'm emotionally conflicted

And hurt

As if I had just been tackled

How could I ever break your heart?

I ask myself this question

Maybe it was selfishness

I definitely played my part

In the destruction

The Ultimate Moment- No Regrets

Of what we established

Which now unfortunately

Has become past tense

Which is the biggest challenge

I love him

And I love you

But even I know

With that kind of situation

There can never be balance

Let me reiterate

I love you

You deserve the best

This I totally understand

Soulmates

God has the perfect plan

As well as the upper hand

Please be patient with me

As I struggle to compose myself

I'm wiping my face as I write this

Only because it hurts

And my eyes

They squirt

I've never felt this way in my life

One of these days

I hope to become a fine wife

But that timetable is open

I'll keep my word

I just need ample time

To sift through these dark clouds

Of troubled sadness

And when I return to your warm embrace

Nothing will ever come between us

You better believe this

Because I'm going to show you

In so many ways

Demonstrate

How much woman is maintained

Within my frame

My heart pumping feverishly

And fluttering

My speech stuttering

Because it will be your love and understanding

That will mean so much to me

It's never too late

The crowd went into uproar of applause. I smiled and waved out to everyone while trying to find Troy within the crowd. I was so overcome with emotion. When a man reached out and grabbed my hand, I was excited with the anticipation of it being Troy. When I looked up it was not Troy who had my hand but Michael. I tried to not show disappointment on my face so I pretended I was happy to see him. I pretended that I was happy that it was him holding my hand.

He pulled me into him and whispered in my ear, "We have to talk." He looked me in my eyes and was very serious.

I nodded to him and told him I understood. But, honestly, I didn't want to talk. I wanted to live in the moment. I wanted this moment shared with Troy.

Jazzaray Harris

After we left Rhapsody, Maxwell and I decided to go eat a late dinner. I said goodbye to the ladies and followed Maxwell to his car.

"Tonight was very interesting. You definitely have some interesting friends."

I laughed and said, "I sure do."

"Boy, it was intense at that table. What have I gotten myself into?" He laughed.

"You must be talking about Dahlia?"

"Yeah. And who was that guy, whatshisname? Oh yeah, Robert. Who was he?"

"Dahlia's ex and Troy's brother."

"Whoa, talk about keeping it in the circle. I saw how he looked at her, kind of how I look at you."

"Oh really? Lord, I see that journey isn't over." I leaned back on my seat.

"So are you ready to talk? It's kind of been on my mind since we left the apartment."

I sighed, hoping that he had forgotten, but I didn't want to hide that part of me, especially since I had a court date coming up. "I struggle with some things."

He pulled into a fast food place and parked his car. "I'm listening."

"I really don't know what to say, Maxwell. I mean I have struggled with this for two years."

He grabbed my hand and held it. "Jazz, I am here and am listening. I promise I will be here for you in whatever it is."

It took maybe five more minutes before I was able to open my mouth. I didn't know how to start. "Two years ago I was involved with someone. We dated for a couple years. Nothing serious but we stayed together, you know. Well, toward the end of our relationship I met someone else. He found out and it didn't end to good. "There's more to the story, right? Tell me why you can't look at the apartment door next to mine."

I turned away from him and looked out the car window. "We never actually broke up. Something happened. Two years ago I was in an altercation. He actually attacked me in that apartment next to yours."

"Wait, are you telling me you were the one? I mean in Terrence's apartment?"

I jumped at the sound of his name. "How do you know his name?"

"I have been in my apartment for three years. I used to know him. It is all making sense now," he said under his breath.

"What?"

He hesitated and turned his body to face me completely. "I was the one who knocked on the door."

"When? What are you talking about?"

"The day that he died. I was the one who banged on the door when I heard a woman scream, when I heard you scream."

I covered my mouth in shock as tears came to my eyes. "That was you? You were the one who was at the door? You are the one who saved my life."

He brought his hands to my cheek and wiped away my tears. "It all makes sense now. The day I met you, why were you there."

In between cries I said, "I was there for relief. I was in therapy dealing with it and they told me to return and release all the pain. I can't believe it was you. Why didn't I see you? Why didn't you stick around?"

"I did, but I never went to see you. I just called the police and made sure they got to you."

Wiping my face, I looked back toward him and said, "I can't believe it was you. I have always wondered who it was at the door that day. And here we are together not even knowing just how connected we are."

He leaned toward me and gently kissed my lips. "Jazz, this moment was meant to be for us. I am madly in love with you."

I looked into his brown eyes and searched for any flaws. I couldn't find any. This man was so perfect. I couldn't believe he was here saying he loved me. I could tell him about my pending divorce, but how was I going to explain Junior? *I have to tell him.*

"I know I love you, Maxwell, but there are a couple things you must know. The reason why I am telling you this now is because it is easier now rather than later." I felt myself get nervous just thinking about his reaction. *What if he says he doesn't want to have anything to do with me? I would truly be crushed.*

"I'm listening." He never took his eyes off me. His attention was focused on me and I knew I couldn't stop now.

I had to say what was truthful and hope for the best. "I have a son. His name is Tim. He is just a toddler and until recently his father and I were together."

"You have a son?"

"Yes," I nervously said.

"Is that it? I love kids. As a matter of fact I have a daughter, she is six."

I smiled at him a little relieved.

"What is her name?"

"Nadia. She is with my ex-wife."

"So you used to be married as well?"

"Wait, you were married to Tim's father. So you are recently divorced?"

I realized that I didn't give the impression that I was married. I did not want him to know that our breakup was more than recent. It pretty much had just happened. Stuttering I said, "Well, we are actually getting a divorce. It isn't final yet."

He sat back in his seat and looked out his window away from me. "So, this is recent. That's a little scary on my end. I know a little how these things go."

"You don't have to worry about that. Our relationship has been over way before we actually said it. Besides, I told him I was in love with someone else."

He turned to me and jokingly said, "Oh really, so I have competition?"

"No, Max." I laughed and shoved his shoulder. "I promise you that my eyes are set in one direction, and I am finally happy with you."

He kissed my lips again. "So when do I get to meet your son?"

"How about we meet our children together? I have a feeling that they will need to get to know each other because you are not going anywhere."

He laughed and started his car. "You're right about that. Plus, I think I have you sprung anyway. How about we rent a room? Knowing the history of my place, I really don't want to take you back there again."

I guess the excitement must have shown on my face.

He laughed and said, "Calm down, we'll rent a room."

We laughed and joked all the way there. I was truly in love with Maxwell.

Dahlia Jones

"I am going to stick around here and chill with Jazz. Me and her haven't spent too much time together. So you go ahead and I will call you when I get home," I lied to Paul straight through my teeth.

He knew I was lying but he left anyway. Well, I assumed he knew that my intentions were to see Robert. Jazz stood there and heard my lie and didn't question me when they proceeded to walk out the door minus me.

My thing was I had two reasons to stay behind: Robert wanted me to, and I knew Nitrah was about to experience hell. The poem she had read clearly told of her love triangle as clear as day. Now was she making a promise to Troy or Michael? I didn't know. My assumption was the first because lord knows she couldn't leave Troy alone. It had been years since Troy and I had that altercation.

But I refused to allow that to make me bitter. I guess it was easier to let go but he and I would never be friends.

I noticed Robert waiting by the back. I signaled for him to give me a moment. I made my way through the crowd, which was still cheering Nitrah on. I saw Michael whisper something in her ear and she didn't look pleased. Why she did that on stage, I don't know.

Getting closer to the two I said, "Hey, Michael, you mind if I speak to Nitrah before I leave?"

"Yeah, might as well." He turned and walked away.

"Where is he going?" I asked Nitrah.

"He's going to go get the car. I got to find Troy before he comes back."

"Don't worry. I am riding with him and Robert. I'll tell him you will call."

"You are riding with them, why?"

"Well, Robert wants to talk."

She rolled her eyes and said, "Again? Well good luck, Miss Diva."

"Before I left I wanted to see if you were okay. That poem, I mean, come on. You were asking for trouble."

"Yeah I know. But I am also tired of playing both sides. I need to decide and maybe tonight I will. Who knows?"

"Call me and let me know how everything goes. This is your night, you need to smile and be happy. Too many people are here for you to be frowning."

We hugged and said our goodbyes.

I later found Robert and followed him to his truck. Troy hopped in the back and I got in the front.

"So, bro, what did you think of Nitrah's poem," Robert said.

"Robert, do not start with me, especially with her in the car."

I rolled my eyes at the sound of his voice. "Don't worry, Troy. I will make sure you keep your image to Fort Worth."

"Calm down, bro. I am just saying it seemed to me she was talking to you."

"Or Michael," I whispered.

"Will you two just shut up and drive so I can get home," Troy said.

"Is Teresa still there?" I said..

"What?" Troy said clearly upset and irritated.

"Dahlia, please don't go there," Robert said.

"Fine, never mind," I said and sat back and folded my arms.

The car ride was quiet the rest of the way to Troy's house. When we dropped him off, his house lights were on. He clearly wasn't there alone.

***

"Now that we are alone I want to get some things across," Robert said. He pulled up in front of my house.

"Let's go inside and talk," I said, opening the door and proceeding to lead the way to my front door.

Inside he made himself comfortable looking around and taking in my new place. Everyone had been here but him.

"This is nice, Dahlia. I am proud of you. You moved out here and have a nice corporate job now. I guess you did move on, huh?"

Sitting my drink down on my table, I said, "Who wouldn't? It was time anyhow. So cut straight to it, Robert. Why did you kiss me tonight?"

He said, "Who wouldn't? Look at you. I'm tired of being the fool who let you go. I want to get back with you. If it wasn't clear, I am making it clear now."

"Why now?"

"It's time. I'm tired of pretending. I'm more than halfway to thirty and I can't understand why I broke it off with you and you did nothing to me. I understand what happened with you and my brother, but I only pray that after all these years we can move on from that and possibly be together."

"It's been awhile you know. I thought when we saw each other at Jazz and Tim's wedding that maybe we could start again. Maybe we just fell into something serious too soon."

"No, I disagree. I don't think there is never a too soon. I just want to live in the moment. So we have done the breaking up and making up. I just want to be with you and I know that."

"How can you be so sure? I mean look at Tim and Jazz, they weren't suppose to end up like this."

Rubbing his temples, he said, "Tim was wrong. But we all make mistakes, and it is just unfortunate that Jazz didn't want to work it out. I know what I want, and I will not leave you again until we have talked it out. I promise."

"I don't know. I am with Paul now."

"Are you serious about that man? Because if so, I will back off and I won't bother you again about this."

"I mean, no, were not serious but he is a fun person."

Robert got up from the couch and walked over to me. "I want to be with you, Dahlia, even if we don't make it this time. I just want to know that I tried and I did not throw something away. I don't want to have to worry about any what ifs."

Breathing in deeply, I thought about everything he had said. I thought of how Jazz and Tim had ended up. I thought of Nitrah's love triangle. I thought of Charmaine's picture-perfect marriage. I told him yes. I didn't have to think about it for long because even with us being separated for so long, we still loved each other as if we had just broken up yesterday. I wanted Robert to be with me. I wanted to finally be happy with just one person, even if I knew this was Troy's brother.

Robert kissed my lips. He pulled my shirt over my head and greedily kissed my breasts, cupping them in his hands. I openly welcomed his hands on my body, wanting to remember the connection we had in the bedroom. We made love that night over and over. For the first time I didn't worry about what was going to happen next. I just released all the worry in my heart and lived in the moment. I loved him and I knew that he loved me. Now if only I could get my girls on track then everything would be fine.

Nitrah Hill

Michael pulled up in his Range Rover then pulled open my door. I waved to the crowd and thanked the owner of Rhapsody for a wonderful night. I hopped in Michael's car, dreading the ride home. He was clearly angry, and I could see his veins pulsating through his forehead.

"You got to be fucking with me, Nitrah."

Rolling my eyes, I said, "What, Michael?"

"What the hell do you mean what? You embarrassed the shit out me tonight. Everyone isn't stupid, they know what you mean on stage. You are fucking off on me. With who, Troy?"

"It was just a poem," I lied.

"What the hell did you promise? Who were you talking to, Nitrah? Do not play with me. I gave you a ring. I proposed to you and this is what you do, embarrass me in front of the whole city of Dallas? I mean the news was there and shit."

Getting irritated, I yelled, "There isn't going to be curse words thrown my way, you need to calm down."

Clearly more hurt than upset, Michael said, "That's all you have to say? After all this, Nitrah, you pull a stunt like that and expect me not to be upset with you?"

"I said it was just a poem. Why are you ruining the night?"

"You still are going to sit there and act like you did nothing wrong?"

Exhaling, I said, "Look, Michael, I love you okay. But for a while now I have been struggling with some things. I mean you and Troy came back in my life at the same time." I stuttered over Troy's name simply because I never say his name to Michael.

Michael looked at me and said, "What the hell does that mean?"

"Michael, pay attention to the road," I screamed.

He swerved out of traffic and hit the curve almost tilting the car to one side. Hysterical, I jumped out of his car, screaming at the top of my lungs. "Are you crazy to be driving like that? What is wrong with you, Michael?"

He got out and walked around to the other side and yelled, "You fucking him, aren't you?" He started to run toward me.

Scared of what he might do, I started to run but slipped over my heels and fell. Before I could get up he was pulling my arm forcing me to turn and face him. He grabbed hold of my other arm and shook me so hard I thought my neck was going to break. He yelled directly in my face as I witnessed his eyes pierced with anger. I had never seen him look at me like this before. He took his hand and grabbed my throat, cursing and spitting on me.

I cried out that he was hurting me. I badly wanted him to let go of me before I passed out. It was starting to hurt. My tears and fear burned my eyes as I cried out for him to stop. As if something or someone hit him in his head, he let go of my neck.

"I. I'm sorry, Nitrah."

Rubbing my arms and crying, I backed away from him. *This is what I get for playing both sides.* He started to back away while holding up his hands to let me know he wasn't going to do anything else.

"I'm sorry, Michael, but I love both of you," I screamed out. My throat was aching.

"Nitrah, I am done. I know you love him but I cannot be in this anymore. I'm sorry for putting my hands on you. I loved you. I wanted to marry you. But I cannot share you. What kind of man do you think I am?"

"I'm sorry. I know what I did is wrong. But you two are so different, I can't decide."

With his head down and rubbing his temples he whispered, "I know you won't be able to, but I cannot share you. If you can't choose then I will for you." He turned around and walked toward the passenger side of his car. He pulled out my purse and walked over and dropped it to my feet. "Here you go and do what you want. I am done."

Touching his arm, I said, "Michael, please don't do this."

"I am not dumb, Nitrah. If you can't choose right off the bat then I must not be it for you. He looked at the ring on my finger and said, "Keep it." He leaned in and kissed my lips. As he walked away he didn't look back. He got in his car and drove off.

I picked up my purse and looked around to see where I was. *I can't believe he left me out here. Maybe I deserved it.* I pulled out my cell phone and called a cab. I was too embarrassed to tell anyone that Michael had left me in the middle of an empty shopping center.

***

When I got home two hours later, I fell across my bed and cried into my pillow. *I knew reading that poem would be trouble.* I slowly slipped out of my shoes and my dress and threw them across the room. I held my hand up and looked at the ring on my finger. The large diamonds sparkled in the moonlight as tears fell down my cheeks. Michael was gone. I could not believe what had happened tonight. I played the messages on my machine but they weren't from anyone I wanted to hear from. I didn't even want Troy to call. I needed time tonight to soak in my tub and just feel sorry for myself. I grabbed a bottle of wine and did just that.

***

The next morning I rose up still in the same position I was in when I had fallen asleep. I looked in the mirror and saw the puffiness in my eyes. I grabbed a towel out of my closet and ran hot water over it. My phone began to ring but I was still not interested in talking to anyone so I let the machine get it. I heard Jazz's voice scream through the phone:

"Nitrah, answer this phone. I know you ain't over there sleep. Get your ass on this phone. I got good news."

Regretting hearing any news at all, I slowly walked over to the phone and pressed the speaker button. "Yes, Jazz, what is it?" I said dryly.

"What's up with you? Never mind I asked because when you hear this, you are going to scream."

"Jazz, why are you talking so loud? Just say it already." I had a headache from crying all night long and her high tone was not helping.

"Anyway, my lawyer just called me. And not only did I win my case but guess how much money Terrence's family has to pay me?"

Taking the towel off my eyes, I said, "You won! How much, girl?"

"Two hundred and fifty thousand dollars."

The towel slipped out of my hand and I repeated the dollar amount.

"Yes, girl, they got to pay me. The best part is that the state is liable for $111,000 and they have to pay the rest out of the trust Terrence had. They are paying me all my money in two checks."

I ran over and grabbed the phone and screamed into the receiver forgetting I had a headache, "Jazz, you are lying."

"No, now get your ass over to Maxwell's house right now. We are going out to celebrate."

"Maxwell's house? I thought he stayed in those ugly-ass apartments."

"No, Miss Thang, he went and bought a three hundred thousand dollars home and not only did he do that, he offered for me and Junior to stay."

"He did, what did you say?"

"I declined because I want to take it slow. Plus, Junior doesn't need to be living with someone else already."

"Did you tell Tim?"

"I haven't had a chance to tell him anything just yet. I already filed and the papers have been drawn. All we have to do is sign."

For some reason I felt like confessing what happened last night. "Michael and I broke up."

"You did, why? It was because of last night."

"Bingo."

"You tell Troy?"

"No. I didn't feel like talking to anyone until you called screaming in my phone. I can't believe how much life has changed for you, Jazz."

"I know, me either. Just a couple months ago I was depressed, in therapy, and in a horrible marriage. Now look at me."

"As fine as Maxwell is I am sure you are doing fine." I teased.

She giggled and said, "Yeah, he is a keeper. But you won't believe this."

"What?" I said. I knew she was about to tell me some gossip.

She recanted the story over to me of how she discovered Maxwell was the one who was knocking on the door the day Terrence had died. I covered my mouth in pure surprise but then it all made sense. He was next door and clearly was able to hear everything that day.

"Wow, Jazz, I can't believe this. It's like Maxwell was sent to you… even after Tim."

"I know. And Lord knows I loved Tim, I still do. But loving and being in love is two different things. I mean even after the fact he is still here. He comes to see Junior every day and on weekends he comes and gets him."

"That's cool and all, but how will he react to you winning the suit and being with Maxwell?"

"I honestly don't know, but I am going over to him today for him to sign these papers before he finds out. Not that I am not trying to hide the money, I don't want him to delay this thing because I have moved on. I don't want to take any chances. Plus, I plan to give him some money just because he did use to be there. Regardless if he fucked Monica or not, our relationship was going to cease anyhow. We stopped trying to be in a marriage. Plain and simple."

"So, with all this money you got now, can I borrow a dollar?" I teased wanting to change the subject. I had just realized that Jazz was moving on and letting go but I was still stuck on stupid.

"Well I do have plans for it. With you opening up the new poetic spot and having that open building next to it, I was thinking of opening a bookstore. Selling nothing but African American books and hosting all kinds of events, you know? Like a collaboration thing. My hours will end at like six."

"Girl, that is a good idea. I don't know why I didn't think of it. Well, my place has its grand opening in two weeks. Let's work out some details. I'm getting dressed now shoot me Maxwell's address to my cell phone."

"Okay, see you when you get here."

We hung up the phone and I prepared myself to go visit Jazz at her new beau's house. Excited about the new direction Jazz and I were going, I pulled on some jeans and a shirt, placed my sun glasses on to hide my puffy eyes, and hopped in my car.

Troy Washington

Just yesterday I witnessed Nitrah spilling her heart in front of everyone. I wasn't sure if it was to me or Michael, but she didn't call my phone just yet to let me know. I was glad when Robert called me and said that we were going to go play basketball at the community center. I needed to clear my head. He invited a few of the guys like Tim, Bobby, and Lesters who were Tim's friends from work. It seemed one way or the other we all had problems. This was our therapy.

"So what's up with everyone? I see you all got a little aggression going on. No ladies here, no enemies are here, it's just us guys," Robert yelled out while passing me the basketball.

"Shit, do we have to talk like we are females?" Lester said.

I said, "Well, I do want to know what happened last night. I did want to be there for Nitrah, but you know what's going on between Jazz and I."

Robert had this corny grin on his face and I knew it must have been because of Dahlia.

"Naw, man, did you hit that again?" I yelled out to Robert.

Trying to act innocent, he said, "What are you talking about?"

"Dahlia is what I'm talking about. I can't believe you went back to her. I knew you were."

"You and Dahlia, again?" Tim said.

"Which one is Dahlia, the fine-ass female with the big-ass mouth?" Lester said.

"Yeah that's her; she is Nitrah's friend and a very distant ex of mines," I said as Lester laughed out.

"Yeah, I talked to her last night," Robert said.

"Yeah, looks like you did more than talk. Wasn't she with ole boy last night anyhow?" I said..

"Yeah, that's over now."

I laughed out and said, "Yeah, whatever, bro." Tim interjected and said, "So, was Jazz there?"

As if Robert and I were reading each others mind, we forgot to answer the question, hinting to Tim that she was and we didn't want to say with whom.

"So she was there with somebody, huh?"

"Man, I ain't in it," Robert said, holding up his hands.

"We suppose to be boys and y'all didn't tell me she was there with someone else. You know she showed up over to the house with the papers and told me to sign. No wonder she was such in a hurry."

"Did you sign it?" I quizzed.

Dryly he said, "Yeah. So now I ain't got Jazz or Monica."

A little disgusted at his statement, I proceeded to dribble the ball trying to act as if I didn't just hear him.

"So what happened to Monica?" Lester said.

"Dahlia got the job to transfer her to Greensboro. The last time I saw Monica was when she was cussing me out and calling me everything in the book."

"North Carolina?" Robert said.

"Yeah, in North Carolina." I nodded.

Lester more curious than anyone else said, "Why was she mad at you?"

"I told her that I told Jazz and that I wanted to be with Jazz. But of course, as you all know, Jazz doesn't want to be with me."

I mumbled, "I can see why."

Tim shot me a look that meant he wanted to connect my face with his fist. "What you say?"

"I said I can see why. You had everything and you let it get away for some pussy."

Tim stepped over to me with so much anger it caused Robert to jump in between us.

"Fuck you, dude. You act as if your ass ain't still cheating. You were worse off than me."

"But I wasn't married, and you cheated at one of the lowest points in that girl's life and now you upset. Man, please. You need to go somewhere with that bullshit."

Tim pushed Robert out the way but he made his way back in between us. I wasn't trying to fight Tim, I just wanted him to see how wrong he was. Yeah I had done some dirt but I know if I had what I wanted, I wouldn't let it go.

"Troy, I will whup your ass. Know that and believe it."

Grabbing my gym bag and walking away I said, "Don't take it out on me, Tim. We like brothers, and I am not going to let you use me as the source to release your frustration. Don't fuck with me and I won't fuck with you. But know this: you messed up. You got married and had a kid and when things got hard, you went back to your old ways. Now I am saying this man to man. What's done is done. She moved on and now you got to move on as well."

Clearly upset, Tim walked off without saying a word. Since Tim was his ride, Lester yelled out a goodbye and ran behind Tim before he drove off.

Robert said, "I didn't invite y'all out here to beef. Man, come on, let's go."

***

After Robert dropped me off, I went into my house to find the kitchen smelling of burnt food. *What the hell is going on?* I rushed inside the kitchen trying to find something that could cover a fire when I saw Teresa. "Teresa, what the hell are you doing in my kitchen burning up shit?"

"My bad, beau, I was trying to surprise you with a meal. I knew you were probably out with the boys."

I went over and turned off all the burners and threw the skillets in the sink and poured cold water over them. "Teresa, I thought I told you that I was done and that we were done. Now you are in my house cooking food that was clearly poison."

"Yeah, I heard what you said but I saw Nitrah the other day with Michael, and it don't seem like she looking for you, beau." She brought her hand to my face and I slapped it away.

"Teresa, don't touch me. Get your shit and get out. This is ridiculous. I didn't take you for some psycho bitch."

"Bitch?" She looked hurt.

"Look, I am sorry; I didn't mean to say that. But come on, you keep pushing me to the limit. Just get out please. And for once, don't come back."

With tears running down her cheek, she turned and grabbed a bag and walked out my front door.

Damn, I got a case of fatal attraction on my hands. I made a mental note to not even risk staying here and planned to find a realtor to move as soon as I could. Until then, I was changing the locks. I walked to my bedroom after dead-bolting my front door and pressed Play on my answering machine.

I had a few messages from family. Mama called and said she was having a barbecue and told me to tell Robert. I thought the barbecue would be a perfect opportunity for Nitrah to meet the family. A few more messages played and then Nitrah's voice came on:

"Troy, we need to talk. I got something to share with you, and I would like to do that before my grand opening up here at the club. Meet me there today whenever you get the message. I'll be there waiting."

I jumped in my shower and dressed in record time. I knew she had made a decision because before she hung up she said, "*I love you, beauty.*"

***

I drove up in front of Nitrah's club and parked. I stepped out and noticed that there were dim lights on inside. I walked up to the front door and it was locked. I knocked lightly on the door but there was no answer. So I walked around the side of the building near the patio area and saw the side door opened. As I neared I could hear slow music playing. I peeked my head inside and still didn't see Nitrah. I quietly opened the door just enough for me to squeeze my body through. As I looked around I saw that everything in the club was completed.

There were luxurious chairs all through the club. The stage had a DJ table and microphone. The bar was fully stocked and small crystals decorated the bar. The barstools were clear and shaped like icicles. The marble floors were newly buffed and shined, and the chandeliers dangled from the ceiling. The scenery was almost breathtaking. I was proud of what she had done here. It definitely screamed high-class. Walking toward the stair rail, I heard small voices. I got excited at the thought of seeing her. Well, that was until I heard her voice along with someone else's.

I went up the stairs two at a time. When I got to the top, I couldn't believe what I saw.

Nitrah Hill

I had prepared a special evening for me and Troy. I hadn't had the nerve to call him since the celebration at Rhapsody last night. And after spending all day with Jazz at Maxwell's new place, I was suddenly determined to make a choice. Well, Michael helped me make that choice. So I knew I had to get some paperwork done at the Lyrical Lounge, plus I had to get an article into Sistah Lit. Magazine. I knew if I left a message for Troy to meet me, I could have everything set up with sensual music playing to help us get into the mood.

When six o'clock rolled around, I figured it would take Troy longer than I thought to get the message. My hopes were answered when I heard the front door open. I walked out of my office and peeked around the corner to see the main entrance and there Michael stood.

"Michael," I called out.

He turned and looked toward me and said, "Nitrah, I knew I could find you here."

My guard went up because I didn't know what he was here for. He reached out his hand and in it was a piece of paper.

"What's this?"

"Read it."

I took it into my hands and opened it slowly. It was a sheet of notebook paper that had the words *I'm sorry* written on them.

"What's this for?" I said.

"I couldn't get over how I left you out there like that. If something had happened to you, I would have never gotten over that. For that I am sorry."

I sat the sheet on one of the tables and sat down. "Thanks, I appreciate it."

He sat down across from me and started to look around. "The club came out perfect. I can't see it any other way."

"I couldn't have done it without you, so thank you so much."

He looked me in my eyes. He was clearly sad. The look in his eyes made me feel so guilty.

"I'm sorry, Michael."

"Nini, I am okay."

I giggled at the nickname. "No, let me speak. I'm sorry for doing this, making us turn out like this. I didn't mean to hurt anyone in this situation. I was just torn between the two."

"I knew you were in love with him. I just wanted to make you forget that you were. I didn't help the situation either. You're a good woman, Nitrah; it's just bad timing for us. I didn't meet you first and even now I didn't get your heart first. Being away in Atlanta all that time I still couldn't get you out of my head. But what can I do? I tried to make you love only me."

"I did at one point, but it just seemed like I could never get away from my past."

We sat there quiet for about five minutes when I said, "You want to see the rest of the place."

"Yeah, guess I can do that."

I went over and locked the front door and he followed me upstairs as I showed him things and pointed to other stuff. He seemed to be excited just as I was. Opening day was only two weeks away. When we reached the top, we admired the paintings I had a local artist place on the walls. Michael stood close to me and placed his hand on the small of the back. I nervously looked at him.

He said, "I am very happy for you, Nitrah." He leaned in and kissed my lips.

I stood there and allowed him to kiss me so softly as if he wanted to cherish my lips on his.

Then I heard a man yell, "Nitrah!"

Michael and I jumped and turned around to see Troy standing there.

Oh my goodness what am I going to say now?

"Is this what you asked me to come and see?" Troy said.

"Um, no, Troy. Look, Michael and I—Lord, I don't know what to say."

"Nini, you don't have to say anything to him. Troy, you are clearly why this woman and I cannot be happy. Why don't you just walk your ass right back out that door."

"Man, I am this close to beating your ass. You came in on my girl after I was with her. We were supposed to be boys."

"I would rather be with her than to be affiliated with your ass," Michael said.

"What you done went and got all corporate on me now? Did you forget that me and you grew up on the same south side of Fort Worth?" Troy yelled out.

I nervously watched what I did not want to happen ever again. That was to have them both in the same room.

Troy walked over toward Michael and pointed his finger directly in his face. "You better walk away before I do something you will regret."

Michael angrily slapped his hand away, which started a small scuffle. Troy reached out and punched Michael in the jaw and

Michael returned a jab to Troy's stomach. I fell back on one of my couches after being pushed back.

"Stop! Please just cut it out."

They both jumped at the sound of my screams. They pushed one another away and stood across from each other breathing heavily with fury.

"I can't do this anymore. Look, we all know what's going on here. I love you both but until I can choose, I cannot be with either of you. I can't do this to you or myself."

"What? Come on, Nitrah?" Troy begged in pure disappointment. Hurt was on his face as he listened to me break my promise. "What about what we promised each other?"

"I can't right now. I just can't. I need you two to just leave me alone," I screamed out again, placing my hands over my ears as if I were blocking out a loud noise.

Michael walked past me without saying a word. He stomped down the stairs and angrily opened the front door and let it slam behind him.

"I can't believe you, Nitrah, yet again we are at this point." Troy turned and walked away.

When I heard the door open and close, I collapsed on the floor and cried. What I had just witnessed was what I never wanted to. The two men I loved most in this world fighting over me.

Dahlia Jones

September 2004

"It sure is nice to have us here all together and just hanging out," Jazz said.

"You sure is right about that. Tomorrow night is the opening of the Lyrical Lounge and you know, Miss Nitrah, is going to be crazy busy with the place, so this is going to be our last hang out for a minute," I said.

"Not only that, ladies, look at how much things have changed in these short months. Jazz is divorced, well pending divorce; Dahlia is back with Robert, which we thought would never happen; I am married, nothing new there; and Nitrah has quit teaching and now owns her dream. I am proud of you ladies." Charmaine toasted.

"Did you forget that I am a marketing director now and I helped my girl here get rid of the bitch who fucked her man?" I said.

Nitrah rolled her eyes and teased. "Such vulgar language."

Jazz laughed out and said, "Yeah whatever, she said it right."

"Yes, Dahlia, I forgot to mention the ass kicking to Greensboro. Oh yeah, isn't Joyclyn going back to school too?"

"Yeah, I forgot to mention that. She is going back to school and Mama and her are on good terms now. Now don't get me started on my brother Zachary."

They all rolled their eyes and I said, "Girl, we know his uptight ass ain't doing nothing."

"So, Nitrah, are you excited about tomorrow night? I mean the whole city is talking about this, girl. Fort Worth doesn't have a club on your level," Jazz said.

Nitrah giggled and said, "Hell yeah, I am nervous. I am sitting here trying to not let the wind mess up my new hairdo because I have to look fly tomorrow night."

"Girl, please, they will be looking at me not you." Dahlia teased.

"You both are lying because when they see Maxwell on my arm, all eyes will be on us," Jazz said.

"Charmaine, you sure are quiet over there, is anything wrong, girl?" I said.

"No, just listening to you all."

I rubbed off my suspicion and said, "Well, Nitrah, have you heard from any of your guys?"

Laughing, she said, "Why you make it sounds like that? And no I haven't. I have actually enjoyed the time to be alone and think. Plus, with my sisters Raven and Tierra in town, I had some distractions."

"Oh yeah, I forgot they were here. So I invited everyone I know for tomorrow night, and I am so excited about announcing the bookstore that will be next door," Jazz said.

"Yeah, I am excited too. We are about to do some big things, Jazz," Nitrah boasted.

"Girls, I am honestly in a good place right now and seeing us all so happy makes it all the better. I mean Robert and I have been on cloud nine. He is so different and so kind. I am not letting him get away this time. I promise to be on my best behavior."

We all laughed out and yelled, "Yeah right."

"Hey, ladies, I got to get home. I will see you all tomorrow night," Charmaine said, getting up from the table and hugging us all before she left.

Her mood did not sit with me right.

"Was it me or is something up with Char?" Jazz said.

"No, something is up, but I didn't want to say. I mean it's Char, she always got everything in order," Nitrah added.

"No, something is going on with her and the more we talked the more quiet she got. I mean she didn't talk much. I do admit we were all stuck on what's new in our lives and all. But, damn, she could of at least acted happy."

"Maybe we should ask her," Nitrah said.

"It's Char, she is never crying on our shoulder; it's always the other way around," Jazz said.

"Damn, you sure are right. Maybe that's our problem. When have we ever asked what's up with her?" I said.

We looked at each other as if we were waiting for one another to answer the question. Our mood had totally changed when we realized that Charmaine was a best friend to us but we hadn't been one to her.

Jazz said, "Great, now I feel like shit right before my opening day," Nitrah said.

"Let's bring it up after the celebration."

I said, "Yeah I agree."

With that we finished our chat and went our separate ways. But secretly we were all thinking the same thing. What was wrong with Charmaine?

Nitrah Hill

I looked my best in black, so when I bought my dress to wear to my grand opening, I knew it would be black. I wore my hair in loose curls all around. My new hair length added a bounce to it that I loved. I wore light makeup to take away the shine in my face, and I carried a small pocketbook. I didn't want to go to my opening alone, but I knew that was going to be the case tonight. None of my girls were single and I didn't want to look like a tag along. So I rented a limo, hopped in the back, and told them to play *Conya Doss* all the way there. I stayed positive and tried to not seem too nervous. I trusted Jazz with setting up everything and helping the party get started so I could make a grand appearance.

When the limo turned onto the street, I saw nothing but a full street of cars. Spotlights were everywhere and I could see many heads from a distance. I eagerly waited to step out the limo and greet my guest. When the limo neared, I heard an uproar of people cheering and clapping. I suddenly became so nervous I felt weak in the knees.

"She is here," someone yelled out.

Channel 4 news was there doing media coverage and so was the editor of Sistah Lit and Essence Magazine.

Lord, please do not let me step out and fall on my face.

The limo stopped directly in front of the entrance to the club. I saw a red carpet laid out. I silently thanked Jazz for the idea.

The limo driver stepped out and the cheers grew louder. I could see people crowding the limo trying to get a closer view. I grabbed my pocketbook and prepared to step out. The driver opened the door and a roar of applause let out as I waved to the crowd. I shook hands and kissed cheeks as I made my way to the front door.

I heard from afar "Hey, Miss Superstar."

Dahlia ran up to me wearing a stunning gold dress that showed every curve she possessed. She grabbed my arm and walked me down the carpet as if I were the bride and she were the groom. She whispered in my ear, "You look sexy, Miss Lady. Work it out. You won't believe who all is here."

I felt my stomach do a backflip as I grew nervous, but I kept my composure and proceeded to greet the crowd. Before I walked in, I turned around and yelled out, "Everyone, have a great time tonight. Thanks for coming out."

Dahlia and I walked in together to meet more people. I kissed more cheeks and shook more hands. I heard a male voice say over the music, "Well well well. I see this is why you can't call a brotha." I turned around and saw my ex Kenneth.

"Oh my goodness, Kenneth, hey." I reached out and gave him a quick hug. He looked fine as hell and just the thought of him in my bed raced through my head. I quickly let go of the image.

"Damn, baby, you sure is looking good tonight. I see you have come up."

I brushed the baby comment off and said, "Yeah, I am trying to do a little something something."

Dahlia pulled my arm and yelled, "Hi, Kenneth. Bye, Kenneth."

I waved goodbye as she pulled me away.

"Lord, Dahlia, I could of least spoken to the man."

"Not in this lifetime. I should get security to kick his ass out. Anyway, you go and socialize with the people. I'm going to go find Robert. By the way, Jazz is standing near the bar waiting for you."

I did just that, talking and explaining my dream to so many people I didn't know. My newly hired staff was taking orders and sending drinks out. I was also excited about some local talent I had performing. The night was going so well I didn't realize that a man was approaching me.

"Your name is Nitrah Hill, right?"

I turned around and I just knew I was seeing a ghost. "Oh my goodness, when did you get here?" I jumped into his arms and tried to keep from getting emotional.

"Just today. You know I had to come support my girl. Damn you look good."

"Yeah and you look rich." I joked.

Denim was wearing a very expensive suit, platinum earrings, a nice platinum chain, and shoes I couldn't even pronounce.

"I haven't seen you in like forever," I said.

He leaned in and hugged me again as if he wanted to make sure he was actually looking at me. "Damn, Nitrah, it has been too long."

With teary eyes I said, "I can't believe you are here. I haven't seen you in a year. You just went off and started working for Swisha House and left little ole me."

"What can I say, being a DJ paid off. Plus, you know you broke my heart." He teased.

I shyly pushed his shoulder and said, "Denim, please."

A camera man came up to us and said, "Excuse me, but aren't you the producer Denim O?"

"Yeah, but this is my girl's night. Don't bother me with any questions."

"Oh no questions, sir, but can we get a photo for the magazine."

"Which one?" Denim quizzed.

"*Essence*."

"Yeah that's cool. Make sure you get a good shot of my girl here." Denim wrapped his hands around my waste and we posed for the camera.

The camera man walked off thanking him for his time.

"Denim O., huh? I can't believe little Denim is a celebrity now."

"Naw, Nitrah, I mean look at you." He turned around and threw his hands in the air. "The Lyrical Lounge. This is hot, boo. You did it all by yourself. I am surprised you didn't ask me for any money."

A little annoyed by the comment, I said, "Why would I?"

"Never mind I said that. But here, I wanted to help support your dream. Anything you need just let me know." He pulled out a piece of paper from his suit pocket and handed it to me.

I turned it over and it was a check. I whispered, "Fifty thousand? Denim, I can't take this."

He told me to be quiet and took the check out of my hand and placed it in my pocketbook. "After everything I did to you, you definitely can take this and use it for anything you want. There's more where that came from if you need it."

I didn't protest as he slipped the check into my pocket book. "Does Mama know you're here?"

"No, but I plan to see yours and mine before I leave, you know."

"You should have told me, we could have thrown a party or something. Like we used to."

"Don't worry about that. Tonight is your night. Look at all these people here praising you. We both made it. We both made our dream come true. I just hope we do right with it."

"I guess your're right. It's just surreal to be talking to you. We really don't talk anymore, not even by phone," I said.

"Yeah I know. I just had to get you out of my system. Now seeing you, I see I still got to work on that."

Rolling my eyes playfully, I said, "Oh please, I am sure you get plenty of comfort now and don't even think about me."

"Oh hell naw, is that Denim?" I heard Dahlia's voice over the music. "Jazz and Char, come here. Guess who done showed back up in the funk we call Fort Worth?"

Jazz and Char along with their dates walked over toward us through the crowd and said, "That's Denim over there looking all debonair."

Enjoying the praise, Denim walked over to them and gave them each a hug. "Ladies, I see I'm not on you all's shit list anymore."

We all laughed and agreed that he was old news. Robert, Bobby, and Maxwell introduced themselves as well.

"Well, ladies, they have turned on the hip-hop. Time to go shake our butts." Charmaine cheered over the music. She grabbed Bobby's hand and pulled him closer to the dance floor. Jazz and Dahlia followed. Raven and Tierra came up to me and congratulated me and spoke to Denim for a while. I sat back and took in the sight of my dream. People were mingling and dancing, drinking alcohol and cheering the DJ on. I was very proud.

"Nitrah, Jailen is finally here, and he showed up with two women on his arm," Raven said.

"What?" I said, clearly embarrassed.

"Don't worry about it. We are going to take care of it," Tierra said.

Denim laughed and said, "Leave the man alone. At least it's only two."

I laughed and said, "You are such a man."

He grabbed my hand. "Well, let this man show you how to dance on the dance floor."

That's just what we did. We danced, partied, and drank until it was after three in the morning and most of the people had cleared out. My girls were already gone to the house drained and tired. I enjoyed the night too much. I lent my sisters my house keys to stay there.

When the last people walked out the door, I locked it and turned around and exhaled. "What a night," I said to Denim.

"Hell yeah, it's almost four in the morning now. I am tired as hell. Whew, this place is trashed. Who are you going to have do the clean up?

"I am. Tomorrow."

"What? I will take care of it. I'll hire a crew to come out." He pulled out his phone and called his assistant and gave him orders to have someone to come by and clean. When he was done he said, "I guess your driver didn't wait."

"I guess not."

"Well I guess you can roll in my Porsche. I don't want to leave you stranded."

"Porsche? Yeah right. You are going to let me drive that sucker." I giggled and grabbed his car keys.

***

The car had so much power, I was afraid to push on the gas too hard. The entire ride Denim was nervously yelling in my ear, "Nitrah, slow down."

"I got this, calm down."

Sitting back more relaxed, he said, "So how has everything been since you know?"

Rolling my eyes, I said, "Since what, Denim?"

"I didn't want to bring it up last night, but I just want to make sure you are alright."

"After a year? Please, you aren't too concerned."

"Are you with him?"

"No, yes, I mean I don't know."

"But you told him."

"Told him what?"

"You know what, Nitrah. Did you tell him about the baby?"

"Part of it."

Rubbing his temples, he said, "What part, Nitrah?"

"The part where it died."

"What? Why did you do that? The man has a right to know."

"Because I wasn't ready to tell him yet."

"So are you two, you know, getting back together at least?"

"I'm working on it. I'll let you know. Maybe."

"I went to see her two months ago. She has gotten big."

"Yes, Denim, I know this. I see her every month. I am bringing her home for good in the next couple months. It's time and I am ready to tell everyone."

"Oh really, even the triplets."

"Triplets?"

"Jazz, Char, and Dahlia!"

"Yes, even them. They will accept my decision eventually. I regret it. But I do want to thank you for not telling anyone."

"It was easier to do when I didn't call. So when are you going to tell Troyon?"

"Lord, you are asking too many questions."

"Yeah I am because you have been holding this secret too long. Nina knows you're her mother, and she needs to know Troyon is her dad. She is still young enough to learn who he is. Do it before it's too late."

"I am, Denim, I am. Before the week is out."

"I am not trying to be hard on you, Nitrah. I just want you to do this and move on. Having a child isn't a bad thing. If you want me to, I'll be Nina's father."

"I'll tell you what I come up with."

The Ultimate Moment

Nitrah Hill

The following day I went to the Lyrical Lounge and found it spotlessly clean. I was there to do some paperwork and count last night's revenues. I astonishingly took in almost twenty five thousand. I was a little disappointed to see neither Michael nor Troy there. It weighed heavy on my heart as I tried to do some accounting. My mind wasn't there. I couldn't concentrate until I made my final decision.

I knew everything Troy and I went through and I wondered if that was something I wanted to continue. Then I thought of

Michael and how much he loved me and treated me like a queen. But would he accept my past and my secret with Troy? I knew I had to make a decision, and as a woman who was about to bring a person she brought into this world home for good, I needed to tell the man I loved.

I dialed his number and it rung three times before he answered and said, "Hello."

"Hey, it's me. I need to come and talk to you."

"Now?" he said.

"Yes now, and I have made my decision about what I need to do and I need to tell you in person."

"Fine, you know where I am."

I locked up the lounge and drove eighty miles per hour on the highway all the way to his house. When I arrived I was nervous. The walk to his front door felt as if the ground was moving beneath my feet. I lightly knocked twice on his door.

He swung it open and said, "Come on in."

"Hey Troy, thanks for meeting with me. I know it's been a couple weeks and I haven't called or gave you an answer, but I needed time to focus on my club and me."

"Yeah, I saw it on the news. You and Denim looked great," he said sarcastically.

"Look, I came here to talk, okay?"

"I'm listening."

"I gave you a promise and after struggling with what happened between us and our past, I finally just want to live and stop worrying."

"So what's your point?"

"My point is, Troy, that I am done. I want to be with you, and I want us to be together until, well—until the Lord calls us to glory."

With a little excitement in his voice, he said, "Are you serious?"

I smiled and said, "Yes I am."

He walked over to me and kissed me passionately on the lips. I took all of him as he greedily connected my mouth with his.

"Nitrah, baby, I am so happy that this is over."

"I have one more thing to say, Troy. Please sit down for this."

"Okay, now you're scaring me."

"Don't be. Whatever I say, just listen."

"Okay."

We sat on the couch. I turned my body so that I would face him when I spoke.

"Remember the night we went to Hillsboro, the night I told you about the baby?"

Nervously he said, "Yeah, I remember."

"Well, I didn't tell you the whole truth. The reason why I am saying this now is because I want us to finally be together. I want to forgive and forget."

"Right, I agree with you on that."

"I didn't tell the whole truth, Troy. Now please just listen and understand that I wasn't in my right thinking when I did this."

"Nitrah, you are scaring me."

"The baby didn't die."

"What do you mean it didn't die?"

"I had the baby when I went to Houston to stay with my sister for a few months before Jazz's wedding."

"You had the baby?"

"Yes."

In complete shock he said, "Where is it, where is the baby now?"

"Her name is Nina. She stays with my sister in Houston. I see her every month and I am bringing her home."

Standing to his feet, he yelled out, "The baby is alive. Why Nitrah? Why would you hide this?"

"I was ashamed to be pregnant by you, by someone who would just leave me and not say anything before they left. I didn't know what to do. My sister convinced me to just let the baby stay with her until I was ready. I hid being pregnant from everyone."

"Oh my God! I can't believe this is happening."

"I am sorry. I went about this the wrong way. And just seeing you back in the city back in April made me realize what situation I put us in."

"Nitrah, I am going to calm down because I'm viewing this from your point of view. But I want to see my child, and I want us to be a family. That's what I want. That's what I need."

I cried into my hands, not believing the reaction I was getting from Troy. "Let's go now. I will go get my sister from my house and let's go get our daughter."

"Let's go and get her," he said. He jumped up and grabbed his keys.

We raced out the door, and I called my house to tell my sister to get ready because I was going to go get my baby. I couldn't wait for Troy to hold his child. I couldn't wait for us to be a family.

I was finally happy that I had let go of my past and allowed my future to take control. I was happy that finally I did something right. That moment Troy said "let's go get her" was the best moment of my life.

So now I sit here and think about everything that had happened. Remembering the scam, the lies, the deceit, and the fights, I see where we all came from. There was such a thing as forgiving. I forgave Troy and he forgave me. My girls were happy and now with the one they truly loved. And finally I wasn't letting life run me. I just lived it.

So when I first started this story, I asked myself was what me and my friends did in the scam worth it? Would it change our lives for better or worse? I think in the end we can all say it worked out in our favor. It wasn't easy getting there, but in the end I don't have any regrets. That was our moment, the moment I realized what the ultimate no no was.

Epilogue
Charmaine Wright

I was so excited about the new club Nitrah had, but I couldn't help but see Bobby's wondering eye. I had played a part in making my friends happy, but was I truly happy myself? I was married to a wonderful man, I thought. But lately I couldn't help but feel the tension in my marriage. I wanted to help put some spark back into our relationship.

I went to Fredrick's of Hollywood and bought kinky attire, something that I never wear, and went to the liquor store and bought some Merlot. I was determined to get my marriage back on track like it was when we had first gotten married. I refused to end up divorced after only a year. I knew our problems were minor anyhow because we just were lacking the sex drive we use to have.

I planned to give him some of my good loving in a way he would never forget. I got excited just about thinking about it. When I arrived home two hours early because I had taken off from work, I noticed he was already home. I didn't let that spoil my plan because I was determined to surprise him with the new me.

I unlocked my door and the house was quiet. *He's sleep, just perfect.* I went over to the kitchen area and stripped out of my work clothes and jumped into my new cat suit. I placed the Merlot in the freezer to get a little cooler. I put my black pumps on and tip-toed to our bedroom. I tried to minimize the creaks that were coming from the floor so I halted my steps. Then I realized the noise didn't stop. I listened attentively and realized I wasn't the one making the noise.

What the hell is that noise? I walked closer toward the back of the house and the noise grew louder. It was coming from my guest bedroom. I walked over and push open the door to find my husband bouncing between another women's legs.

"Bobby!" I screamed.

He jumped up and immediately started trying to explain.

"You son of a bitch. You sleeping with someone else in our house. Our house!" I looked over toward the bed as Bobby tried to push me out of the room and then that's when I realized who was in my bed. My heart dropped and I was full of rage. I couldn't believe my eyes.

"Joyclyn!" Dahlia's sister was in yet another bed that didn't belong to her.

Reading Group Discussion Questions

1. Do you believe the group of friends matured over the year? If not, who do you think lacked in progression?

2. In Tim and Jazz's relationship, why do you think it was easy for Tim to go back to his old ways?

3. Why do you feel Troy never returned back to his player mentality?

4. Do you think Robert and Dahlia deserve to be together? If not, what do you think should happen to their relationship?

5. Nitrah took a new path in life with her career, where do you see her café going in the future?

6. Why do you think Denim left Nitrah's life, and do you think he will ever stop loving her?

7. Nitrah held the fact that she was pregnant a secret, do you think her secret will backfire in the future?

8. How do you feel about Jazz and Maxwell's connection years prior to them actually dating?

9. In each character's life, what do you think is their ultimate moment, and what do you think they may have regrets about.?

10. What do you think will happen in the third installment of the series, *Will Love Ever Know Me?*

Acknowledgments

First and foremost I want to thank my Lord and savior Jesus Christ. As I try to strengthen my walk with you, you still continue to bless me. Secondly, I would like to thank my husband Marckus who was mad when I didn't write his full name in my last acknowledgement, so I am right now: I love you, Marckus Newhouse. LOL. You are such a great man, and I am so lucky to have met you at 14 and have two beautiful children who take after their mama. LOL.

I want to acknowledge my godmother, my big mama, Charlie Irvin, and my grandparents A.D Harris and his wife. I mentioned a lot of people in my first book so I don't have to mention too much. But I do want to say thanks to my daddy whom after mama left has called a little more than usual. Now that's a huge step for us because time can go by and we not talk for a couple years.

I also want to thank Mrs. Clemis, my step mom, because when I was down and trippin' about this new industry, you talked to me and told me flat out what was going on. I want to tell ya I have gotten smarter I have separated myself a lot from some folks and will stay focused on Gods vision.

Lastly, thanks to my kids, and my sister who has changed her life around. I am so proud of you. I want you to know that mama is not only proud of what your doing but she is still praying that you start to use your spirit of discernment and focus on you. It's your time to shine. So shine so bright that you blind the haters.

To those who beat me to heaven continue to watch over us, and I will pray that when my time comes that not only will I leave a positive mark on earth but that I will party with you up there.

Thanks to all my friends and family and my business associates.

Tamika
Smooches!

Tamika Newhouse is the award-winning author of two novels. She is currently pursuing two bachelor degrees at the University of San Antonio and working hard on her next novel. She currently lives in San Antonio with her husband and two children. She is also on a national book tour, visit her site at www.tamikanewhouse.com. Feel free to call Tamika and leave a personal message at (641) ,715.3900 EXT: 96359

Authoress Tamika Newhouse Fan Club

As a part of the Tamika Newhouse Fan Club, you are exclusively set up to receive many perks that other readers will not have. Get the updated news on Tamika's literary events, book signings, dine and signs, book club meet and greets, and Literary Sistah's tour stops. You are also able to talk to the author through the fan club and get the opportunity to meet her when she comes to your city. As a part of this group, you will have the chance to win free books, exclusive buys, win gifts every month, and you will know first about the author's upcoming events. And you can purchase Tamika Newhouse's novels before the public can. What are you waiting for? Join today by going to the link below.

www.tamikafanclub.ning.com

CPSIA information can be obtained at www.ICGtesting.com
Printed in the USA
LVOW121557211212

312797LV00002B/259/P